BENDY™
THE LOST ONES

BENDY™

THE LOST ONES

BY ADRIENNE KRESS

SCHOLASTIC INC.

All rights reserved. Published by Scholastic Inc., *Publishers since 1920*. SCHOLASTIC and associated logos are trademarks and/or registered trademarks of Scholastic Inc.

ISBN 978-1-338-57221-6

1 2021

Printed in the U.S.A.   23

First printing 2021

Book design by Jeff Shake

The Lost Ones

We all live in a world of make-believe. Let's just be honest about this for a moment. A paradise built on the sand, but we make sure to keep it from the sand with a boardwalk we also built. A paradise by the sea, kept from the sea, as waves crash far below the long, outstretched fingers of piers. We made this. We made cars. We made hotels. We made money.

We made the machine.

We made it.

A decision was made to create, and create we did. Rules. Laws. Social circles. Social strata. It's all man-made. All from our imaginations. From our grand illusions.

It's all just a fantasy.

But it can still destroy you.

The things we make.

They can still kill you.

PROLOGUE: WALLY

Late nights were my favorite time

of day. I liked the empty halls, the darkness, no people running about like chickens with their heads cut off. *It's just a job*, I'd think to myself. *Why do they have to get so worked up over a job?* I liked how my footsteps echoed but I also liked putting on a record or turning on the radio and letting the music play while I emptied trash cans and mopped the floors. Sometimes

I'd do a little dance with the mop. Mop dances are fun. I ain't no Fred Astaire, but then again, he ain't no Wally Franks.

Now that's not to say that there weren't strange things about working late, but if ol' Wally knows one thing, he knows that folks like having their little secrets. Makes 'em feel special. Never understood that myself. What you see is what you get with me.

There were secrets here in Joey Drew Studios. I ain't no fool. But I also ain't no detective.

So I just keep on my own business. Even when the new renovation started, when they'd bought up the theater next door. Even when the pipes had begun making strange noises all hours. Sometimes almost like some creature moaning away somewhere. It was all never mind for me. Made life interesting, new halls to keep up all swell like, new offices, and, sure, new sounds too.

Took more time to clean though, and my muscles did ache more and more these days. The missus always said we should retire down to Florida already, but I wasn't ready yet. Not yet.

"Let me explain this one last time to you thick-headed lunks. I don't want to see one darn scratch on this thing when we get there. Got it?"

"Yes, sir, of course, sir."

I overheard conversations all the time in this job. Not just by being around a corner, or in the other room. No, folks sometimes seemed to forget I could hear in the first place; they'd just talk or argue with me standing right there doing my job.

Ol' Wally didn't mind. Folks did what they did. Just like I did what I did.

So normally I wouldn't have thought too much of any of it, but this time was a bit different. This was, well, I could have sworn that I was listening to the booming frustration of one Thomas Connor. And I could have sworn the fellow had been recently fired. Maybe I was wrong though. Wouldn't be the first time, as the missus always points out.

"Don't 'yes, sir' me. Just do your job!"

And sure enough, it was him, or at least his chest, as I crashed right into him turning the corner.

"What the . . ." Thomas backed off, sputtering.

"Sorry about that, Thomas," I said, casually brushing myself off. Bumping into folks happened sometimes.

"Wally, you're here late," replied Thomas, glancing over his shoulder and not really making eye contact. I rarely got eye contact from folks. I didn't mind it. I didn't want to get in the way. My job was to make the way easier, not harder after all.

"Not really," I replied. Didn't much think he'd want conversation but he didn't walk away so I did my best. Come up with a question, then, Wally. That ain't a hard thing to do. "You're back on the payroll then?"

"What?" asked Thomas. The man seemed distracted.

"Your job, got your job back? Mister Drew hired you again?"

"Well, he had no choice," replied Thomas, still thinking about something else. He laughed then. "We both had no choice."

4

I nodded. I didn't understand what he meant. After all, we all have choices. But folks like when you nod. Sets them at ease.

Thomas turned then and began to walk off into the dark blackness of the hallway. Now I always liked the dark, felt like a cozy blanket to wrap myself in even though I knew others found it scary and such. Never understood that either. Ain't nothing in the dark that isn't there in the light.

Most of the time.

"You moving that machine then?" I asked Thomas's back. I'd just remembered about that now, and felt like asking.

The man stopped walking. He was silhouetted by the last light dangling overhead before everything got drowned in darkness. His shoulders rose, fists clenched. Now there was a man with some anger in him, I observed. Yup, some mighty fine anger.

"Machine?"

"That large machine, the one that makes a mess of ink everywhere." Didn't mind cleaning up, but boy oh boy was it annoying to clean up a messy spill and then it's back again half an hour later.

Thomas didn't turn around. He stood there silent. I figured I should probably stay silent too. I was curious about the answer. I didn't always need one. I didn't always care for one. But I knew when someone needed to answer a question, even if it was more for himself than for the person asking it. Thomas Connor needed to answer this question.

"Yup, we're moving it," he finally said.

"Good," I replied. "Don't know how that thing works, but ever since it arrived there's been ink everywhere. Seems like it's being dragged along the floors by folks. The pipes are also just out of control, leaks and noises, and I've been having a devil of a time fixing the darn things. You know, I don't even understand why this machine exists at all, no one's bothered to tell ol' Wally anything—"

"Yes, well, we're moving it so you'll be happy then," interrupted Thomas curtly.

That made no sense to me. "Well, it's not about my being happy . . ."

"It's done, Wally. It's done."

Now ol' Wally was no fool. There were times you knew someone needed to answer a question and then there were times you knew that the person had answered the question and that was all they were going to say. All that they needed to say.

"Well . . . good then," I said. I touched the tip of my cap. I liked doing that. Wally's salute.

Thomas kept on standing under that one light. I could see the muscles under his shirt tense and relax and tense again. He released his fists and moved his fingers, a bit like he was making sure they still worked or something.

Yes, sir, that man definitely had anger in him.

Definitely.

Then he took a step forward and disappeared into the dark. That's the way it is here at night. Into the light for a moment and then back into the dark. Saving money on electricity, I guessed. Saving money was a priority these days at Joey Drew Studios. I'd been told to keep my rags until they fell apart in my hands. I was good at taking orders, I appreciated them. I'd seen artists reach into their own garbage bins and pull out tossed pieces of paper to draw on the reverse side. I'd seen lunches brought from home. I'd seen pay stubs with lower and lower amounts and empty desks.

I'd seen it all.

I'd seen everything.

Oh yes, ol' Wally sees everything. Including the machine. Including what made the ink on the floors. What dragged it far down the hallways and along the walls.

You didn't think ol' Wally had seen it?

Ol' Wally sees it all.

I went into a small tidy office and picked up the half-full bin. I tossed the garbage into the bag, and paused at the little light on the desk. I leaned over and clicked it off. Saving electricity and all that. Then I went back out into the hallway. And kept going about my business.

Into the light for one moment, then into the dark.

Never much understood why folks were scared of it.

Ain't nothing in the shadows that isn't there in the light.

Except, of course, when there is.

And when there is, I'm outta here!

1: BILL

I pulled my jacket collar up around my neck and crossed my arms tightly over my chest. The air had an unexpected bite to it. There had even been frost on the windows this morning. But did that dissuade Father from his plans today? Oh no.

"What about the girl?" I had asked from my end of the table in our generally gloomy dining room. Light wasn't my father's favorite feature at the best of times, but some young, inexperienced architect had decided that the windows in this part of the house ought to face north. Adding to that, Father didn't enjoy large electrical bills though he could very well afford to pay them, so any artificial help was left unused until after 5:00 p.m. in the fall.

"What girl?" Father hadn't looked up from the paper and stabbed at his grapefruit blindly.

"The horse-diving girl. She'll freeze," I'd said.

Father had shaken his head and stabbed at the grapefruit again. It retaliated and shot back with equal force, covering my father's starchily pressed collar in pink juice. That ended the conversation there as he stormed off to change.

●●●●●●●●●●●●●●●●●●●●●●

To give him credit, his lack of consideration for the horse-diving girl seemed now possibly correct in a way. She stood up there on the diving platform in a white bathing suit and white bathing cap, looking as comfortable as if it was mid-July. I didn't understand how it was possible for her to not be completely cold to the bone, but I respected it. I turned to look at our audience on the bleachers. I hadn't at the time realized just how far Father's pantomime was planned. The hundreds of paid locals sitting in their summer best in the stands made me tug even harder at my own collar. I regretted not bringing a scarf, but at least I wasn't them. At least I wasn't part of the illusion of the day.

I turned and wandered back toward the camera and its operators. I had been shooed off once before, but I thought if I was more casual this time, as if I just happened to accidentally appear directly beside the two men, they might let me watch this time. They weren't filming yet anyway, they were still setting things up. And I told myself this time I wasn't going to ask any questions, I would just observe. I would just . . .

"Scram, kid," said the one holding one of the film canisters.

"But I . . ."

"I said 'scram.'"

I turned on my heel. At least the heat rising in my face from the embarrassment would keep me warm.

I pretended then to have great interest in the diving platform, as if going to check on the camera had been part of a larger scheme to make sure everything was ready for the shoot. I looked back up at the girl standing casually at the top. She looked down at me then and I felt a need to say something, anything. Be reassuring even if she seemed perfectly at ease.

"Everything is just fine!" I said with a wave. She smiled and nodded. She was a sport, that one, replacing her sister last minute like this. I'd never met Constance Gray, but Molly was famous here in Atlantic City and my father had been quite keen to get her. He'd kept the brave face when learning she was sick and her sister would be doing the dive instead.

My father. Such a brave man. Buying up hotels. Investing in nightclubs. All while the war raged on the other side of the ocean. "When these men come back, they'll need to remember what they were fighting for!" Ah yes, and that would be watered-down expensive drinks and girls in shiny costumes then?

This was what this film was for. To remind everyone, not just the men who had returned from war last year, but the women too, and their children, what it was they had sacrificed for. The chance to go on holiday on the seaside! To play games! To eat, drink, and be merry! To watch a girl dive into the water on the back of a horse from over sixty feet in the air!

A "tourist film," Father had called it. Hence the illusion. The height of tourist season was May to August. People came here for the warmth, not the bitter cold wind off the Atlantic in mid-October. So everyone had to pretend it was summer. We'd already done some shots on the beach and Boardwalk last week when it hadn't been nearly as cold. But today, well, today he was most excited about. If anything drew a crowd, it was horse diving at the Steel Pier. Also paying people to attend did that too.

I examined the platform. I was always shocked by its appearance. It hardly seemed safe from an engineering standpoint. A skeletal wood-and-metal frame, bolstered by steel wires attached to the ground. I have to admit that my interests were more mechanical than structural usually (I still really wished someone would let me play with that camera), but all of it still fascinated me. How things were made, how they worked, how pieces of a puzzle came together. I'd walk along the Boardwalk staring at the hotels built at the turn of the century—how did they do that with the old-fashioned tools of their day? The piers jutting out into the water fascinated me as well. They'd stood there against the beating current and the salt for decades.

"That's not normal," I said just then. My eyes had followed the length of steel wire down from the top of the platform to the ground. The bolted metal square that held it in place looked almost as if it had been pried up. A fear welled up from deep inside me.

"Is that normal?" I asked louder, but no one was listening

to me. Everyone had their own tasks to manage. The fear was growing, a panic too. This wasn't good. This wasn't good at all.

No, we had no time for panic. This was time for action. I swallowed the feeling and looked for my father, but he was standing with the director, engaged in one of their regular heated debates. Father liked to fancy himself a creative type who was just too pragmatic to pursue the arts. I glanced over at the editor of the *Atlantic City Press* standing just a little ways off, watching the whole thing go down. Father didn't need any more bad press, but I also had more important things to take care of right now.

I made my way over to a skinny young fellow with red hair and freckles leaning against the stairs up the platform. "Hey, uh, does that look normal to you?" I asked him.

He stared at me, wide-eyed. This happened to me a lot. I didn't feel like anyone of note but I couldn't deny reality. Being the son of Emmett Chambers meant I was my own kind of celebrity. I hadn't done anything. I had just been born to a rich man who owned half of Atlantic City.

"That bolt there, the wire, does that seem safe?" I pointed, and the man turned and looked, thank goodness.

"Uh . . ." he said, and moved toward it. I followed him. We looked down at it, then up at each other. "No, that's not good."

As I thought. The fear churned inside me but I held it at bay.

"Okay, so we should tell someone about it, shouldn't we . . ."

"Steve."

"Steve, we should do something about this."

Steve nodded. "There are some tools at the stables. I can go get those."

"Do that," I replied. Steve ran off at a good speed and I turned and looked at my father. I didn't want to get him involved in this, but if there was something as big as a potentially deadly diving platform with a girl standing at the top of it, he really ought to know.

"Father, we have a problem," I said quietly.

"Not now, William," he replied with that curt clenched-teeth response of his I heard far too often.

"Yes, now, Father."

"What's going on?" asked the director. I wasn't exactly being subtle here and I didn't want to be. People needed to know about the imminent danger.

"A bolt has come loose on one of the wire supports," I said, grateful someone cared. "A fellow named Steve is getting some tools, but maybe we should get Constance down?"

"You sent off the horse boy on some errand when we have a schedule to keep? And who the bloody heck is Constance?" asked my father, seething so obviously even the director looked taken aback.

"The horse girl. She's still up there."

"Definitely not. We bring the girl down, the audience gets up and goes. Fix the darn thing, and do it fast."

"But she's in real danger," I said to his retreating back. That made a few of the other fellows standing around look at me.

My father completely ignored me. Instead he gestured at the young man standing next to the newspaper editor.

"You there!" he called out.

The young man looked over his shoulder and back again. And then pointed at himself.

"Yes, you, stop pointing at yourself like that. Take the horse up to the girl."

I stared in utter confusion. The last thing we needed was a thousand-pound horse on that platform right now.

"Do you understand me?" I heard my father say as I rushed back to the wire. I saw Steve running with his small tool kit, his face as red as his hair. Good lad, Steve. At least someone else understood the gravity of the situation.

"Then do it!" The final order my father gave before I saw him huffing back in my direction. So now he cared. Or now he wanted to take his anger out on someone. It didn't matter.

Steve pulled a giant wrench from his bag and stared at it and then the loose bolt. He looked up at me.

"I'll do it," I said. I was a fairly strong individual, through no effort on my own part. Just another gift given to me by my father. Sometimes I truly despised that I looked like him this much. Steve, meanwhile, looked like a stiff breeze could blow him over.

He handed me the wrench and I heard my father order the other men milling about to surround me. "We have to hide this from the audience," he said. He seemed more concerned about that than the loose wire and the platform.

I hunched down beside the large metal plate and stared up. The platform shuddered dangerously then, and I looked over to see that the horse was being brought onto the platform by the very nervous newspaper fellow. This was complete insanity on my father's part; if we didn't fix the wire, the whole platform could topple to the ground. I looked down as splinters of wood from the pier cracked beneath the weakening plate.

Get to work.

I began trying to wrench the bolt tight again and noticed my hand was shaking just a bit. *Breathe*, I told myself. Just fix it. But even my own considerable strength was not going to be enough.

"Steve, get some men and go to the far side of the platform and push," I said, making brief eye contact with the man before returning to my work.

Once again Steve took me seriously. I could tell because Father was raging: "Where are you going?" To give Steve credit for understanding our dire situation, he ignored my formidable father and soon he and a few other much larger men were on the other side of the platform. I nodded at them from my side, viewing them through the giant wooden beams, and they pushed.

The difference the push made was a matter of inches, not feet, not yards, but inches was all I needed. The metal plate lay flush with the pier and I wrenched the bolt as tightly as I could with my shaking hand, wrenching my own neck in the process. It hurt, but I kept tightening.

"Oh for goodness' sake, boy, it can't get any tighter," my father said, suddenly right over my shoulder. "Get up before some idiot out there figures out what's going on."

I looked up at him. From this angle, his face drooped down even more than usual. He was still an intimidating figure, but from below he looked more grotesque than anything. I returned to the plate but he was right. The whole system holding together this platform was weak to begin with, a cheap way to get a woman on a horse into the sky. But at least the wire was secured to the pier again.

I stood up and Steve and I exchanged a nod. Good fellow, that Steve.

"Right, let's get rolling!" announced my father.

I made my way back behind the cameras and looked up at the girl now sitting on the horse. It was all pretend. All for show. All for the cameras.

And yet there really was a girl on a horse soaring through the sky.

Imagine that.

2: CONSTANCE

It's a long way down to the murky depths. These were the kind of "poetic flourishes," as my father called it, that my brain couldn't help but muster in the most inconvenient times. After all, I had agreed to this. Hadn't I even offered? I wanted to help. Poor Molly was just too under the weather and it wasn't fair to put her through this. And Lily, well, Lily was afraid of horses after all.

Yet here I was, pulling at the corners of my cap, trying to keep warm from the stiff October breeze as I stood there, sixty feet in the air.

"Is everything okay down there?" I called out again. My first attempt had gone unanswered. I arched my back slightly, stretched my neck to see if I could see what was going on in the crowd that had gathered below.

The rich kid finally looked up. He held his hat in place and waved. "Everything is just fine!"

I nodded, but to be perfectly honest, I didn't believe him. What did rich kids know about "fine"? What was a rich kid's definition of "fine" anyway? I figured our fines had to be very different.

But what was I going to do? Climb back down the stairs?

Well, yes, that was a thing I could very reasonably do.

But I wasn't going to. Because I was a "team player." Again, as my father said. I didn't make a fuss. I did what was needed to get the job done. There wasn't space in our little apartment for me to make fusses. Not with Molly's star on the rise, and Lily's particular brand of narcissism. Being promoted to the chorus at the Diamond Lounge was definitely not helping there. No room for Constance to complain. No room for Constance to have much of a personality at all really.

Keep your head down, Constance. Do the job.

Get it done.

I shifted my gaze out toward the stands. They were full, but that had been carefully orchestrated by the rich kid's dad. Mr. Chambers could pay for an audience, and he needed a full audience for his little movie, after all. This time of year, with the tourists slowly thinning out, getting locals to the Steel Pier to watch another horse-diving show was not exactly without its challenges. Add to that that the rider was a nobody who had, at the last minute, replaced her very fabulous somebody sister. Well, when you pay the audience, it's a different kind of crowd is all I'm trying to say.

They were restless. I could feel it even from all the way up here. They were cold too, like me. Mr. Chambers had likely not counted on this northerly wind for his big shoot. And like me they were dressed as if it was summer. No, not quite in their bathing suits and nothing else, but light dresses and linen slacks. I was glad they weren't in bathing suits. Lily always said that when she was nervous, she imagined the audience in their skivvies, but I never understood that. She clearly lacked the secondhand embarrassment gene that I had inherited from Mother.

"Oh dear no, no, don't think of them like that!" she had said in response to Lily being outrageous, which of course was why she was outrageous in the first place.

I said nothing, just kept my head down. I wanted to say that the thought of a whole audience of people, of all sizes and shapes and genders, in their underthings? It made me blush and *more* uncomfortable, not less. No, I was happy to just try to ignore the audience altogether. Fortunately, when one was up on a diving platform as one was now, the distance from the audience was such that you could barely make out individuals.

Just a frustrated mass.

A blob.

An anxious waiting blob.

The platform shook, and I grabbed the metal railing beside me. My stomach lurched into my throat. Was the thing about to collapse, was that what all the fuss had been about? My potential imminent demise. "You mean falling to your death," I heard my father's voice say in my head.

Well, yes, Father, that is what I meant. But I think in fancy words. Even as my life comes to an abrupt end.

I'll tell you one thing: I'm never helping Molly out of a tight spot again, that's for sure. And I'll be haunting the heck out of her.

I looked down the long set of stairs and saw that a young man I didn't recognize was slowly climbing up with Trix in tow. Oh, I see. It was time. The shaking had been perfectly safe. That kind of shake is to be expected, not the kind of shake that, well, isn't.

Trix did look fine. She was brushed to a sheen, her mane blowing in the wind like she knew she was the star. It was likely she did. I always gave too much credit to animals, even Molly said as much, but I just thought, how could they not have feelings and opinions and such? They know us, they recognize us. Surely that ought to mean they like us or don't as well.

Trix was a beautiful, kind horse. She loved everyone. She was Molly's horse but she was so sweet when I rode her, I could tell she enjoyed our time together.

Did she enjoy diving into a small pool of water sixty feet below?

That I wasn't as sure about.

But she never complained.

Kept her head down.

Just like me.

"Hi there!" I said. The young man was so close now, I was feeling a bit strange just standing there waiting. I supposed that was what Molly always did. She was the star, the horse was brought to her. There was no one outside that world. But how can one just ignore a person. Right there.

"Hi," he said. He smiled and I figured he had to be about my age, seventeen or eighteen. But he looked tired, and what was that wonderful term? World-weary, that was the one. Like he had something heavy on his mind.

"Thank you for doing this. I'm guessing Steve didn't show up?" I said. I knew I sounded awkward. I was terrible at small talk.

"I don't know, but they needed someone to help out." He glanced down the ramp and took a step backward.

"I'm like that!" I said quickly.

He furrowed his eyebrows at me. "Like what?"

"Oh, just, when someone needs help, I help. I was meaning to say I appreciate it that you helped. That is, I understand why you volunteered." Why was I still talking? I could tell from his body language he just wanted to get off the platform.

"Okay," he replied. He glanced down again. I followed his look. A small crowd, including the rich kid and his father, was standing at the base of the ramp. "Look, I need to get back down, so do you need help up?"

"Ha, back down, help up," I said. Ah, that was stupid.

"Well, do you?"

"Oh, yes. Yes, I do." I definitely needed help up. I needed all the help I could get. Clearly. Forget the thought of the audience in their underwear making me blush, my own words coming out of my own mouth were more than effective at that. Oh, why couldn't my brain be as articulate outside my head as it was in it?

Trapped in my own brain. That's what it felt like sometimes. All these feelings, these frustrations, just bubbling away, unable to get out.

"So . . . what do I do?" He was getting tired of me, I was taking too long. I wasn't being professional.

"Oh, just hold her steady while I get on. She's a good little lady, she'll be easygoing though." That sounded like a somewhat decent thing to say.

The young man nodded.

"Need any help?" called out the rich kid's father just then. It didn't sound like a real concern. Because it wasn't. It was an instruction: Get on with it.

"I guess we should get on with it," I said.

"I guess."

The young man held Trix's bridle with slightly more conviction than before, and he planted himself in a wide stance. I nodded and quickly climbed up on her back. It was similar to riding bareback, aside from the bumper she wore at her shoulders that attached around her front and prevented me from slipping too far forward when we dove together. It was for everyone's safety, hers and mine, that there wasn't a saddle or reins or stirrups. Once in the water, we needed to break free from each other easily.

"You all set?" asked the young man as I shifted my position slightly.

"Oh yes!" I said, looking down at him. "Yes, thank you so much."

23

"I'll go then?" He seemed unsure. But of course he was—he'd never done this before, I assumed.

"Yes, please!" I was trying now to get into the right head-space for the dive and feeling terribly nervous. I hoped I hadn't sounded curt with my reply.

Oh, dang it all. Maybe I had.

"My name is Constance, by the way?" I said, turning as he started his descent.

He looked back at me. "I know." He turned around once more and I felt like an idiot again, though I honestly wasn't sure why this time. I turned back and leaned down to pet Trix's neck.

"Well, I'm an idiot, aren't I, girl?" I whispered into her ear. She gave a short snort then, and I laughed a little. "You're not supposed to agree."

"Whenever you're ready!" There was the rich kid's father again. I hated to think it, but I was pretty sure at this point I wasn't well fond of him. "We're rolling."

Whenever I was ready, and yet it felt quite the opposite. They were ready. It was time.

Oh boy, was I ever scared.

No, I was supposed to call it nerves. Never scared. "Scared is not the same thing," Lily had insisted. "Scared holds you back. Nerves push you forward."

"Come on, Trix, let's get this thing done. Then we can both go home." She snorted again, and I guided her slowly out farther on the platform so that her hooves were just before the diving ramp. Though one could hardly call a piece of wood that hung out over and down from the platform at a ninety-degree angle facing toward the water a "ramp," exactly.

I leaned into Trix's neck. I felt her mane against my cheek, coarse but warm with that wonderful familiar smell of dry hay. I squeezed with my arms and legs, holding my body as close to hers as I could.

"Okay, Trix, it's time. Let's fly."

I squeezed her sides hard with a sharp single motion, and she stepped out onto the diving board and then we were in the sky. The speed was sudden, and the cold wind rushed around us like it was alive.

It was mere seconds and the water rose to greet us. I closed my eyes.

Keep your head down, Constance. Do the job.

Get it done.

3: BRANT

Let's talk about telling a story.

Let's talk about narrative decisions, and point of view and what you want to say. What you really want to say. Let's talk about shaping public opinion and leading a reader in a particular direction. Let's talk about how even when a story is based in fact and telling the complete truth, it still has its bias. Let's talk about journalism and integrity.

Let's talk about freezing your butt off in the middle of October while some rich folks try to pretend it's not.

Let's talk about horses in the sky.

And girls in bathing suits.

And a crowd of paid spectators cheering on cue.

Let's talk about all these people, and standing right there in the midst of it all and being totally and completely invisible.

Oh yes, let's talk about that especially. How many journalists try to disappear, to observe quietly, get the story, the real story, as if their own personal stories don't affect the words they write? Let's talk about how none of them really know what being invisible is actually like. Being from the wrong side of the tracks, as they say. Not being born to a family of writers. Not growing up with any expectations of going to college. Not graduating from high school.

Just wanting to write.

So you get a job in the mail room of a newspaper instead. You become a quality errand boy. Still they don't see you. But you see everything.

Until they do see you.

"You there!"

Me there? I was shaken from my thoughts. Probably a good thing—they were getting far too full of self-pity for my liking.

I pointed at myself, aware I was me, and aware I was there, but shocked that this large man in a large winter jacket with a large fur wrap could even notice me.

"Yes, you. Stop pointing at yourself like that. Take the horse up to the girl."

I stared at him for a moment. Well, that is to say, I stared in his direction. I was thinking, processing his command. I understood that there was no way he'd know I was there for journalistic reasons, but what on earth made him think I had any horse-taking abilities was quite something else.

"Do you understand me?" He spoke slower now, like he was talking to someone who didn't speak the language, or a child, the way some adults talk to kids as if they are stupid and not just figuring stuff out.

I nodded.

"Then do it!"

Well now, just because I understood didn't mean I had to obey him. I turned to Mr. Clark. "Just do it, Brant. I know, I know. But let's just get this darn day over with already."

"Sir, I'm not crazy about horses," I replied. I said it hesitantly; I wasn't really keen to share this fact about myself. I found it pretty embarrassing, to tell the truth. After all, horses were a part of everyday life, especially here in Atlantic City. Pulling ornate carriages for lovers on the Boardwalk, that kind of thing.

"Just do it, and I'll make it up to you."

"I want a byline," I said quickly. I knew when to take advantage of a moment. That was certainly one thing I was good at. My uncle had instilled that in me when I was little: "You say yes to any opportunity you get. You'd better believe all those other folks are."

"Brant, you know I can't give you that." Mr. Clark shook his head sadly and that weary expression materialized on his face. I saw it a lot more these days. He was a tired man. Well, I wasn't tired, not yet. I was young, I was newly a man myself, had the birthday smacks from my little cousins to prove it. Eighteen and ready to say yes to all opportunities. Maybe not so ready to say yes to horse-based opportunities, but in general. I was more than ready.

"Mr. Clark, I'm not kidding here, I want a byline."

"You're a kid . . ." he said, almost more to himself than anything.

"I was a kid bringing you your lunch. You were the one who saw my potential. Who *really* saw me, didn't see through me like most. I know you see me, Mr. Clark."

"Brant . . ."

"And now, as of two days ago, I'm an adult under the law. And more than that, you've always treated me fairly. I know you see something in me. You brought me here today. To watch you work and learn. So I want a byline. I'll still bring you lunch, I'll still hold your hat, but I want that byline."

He was silent for a moment. I knew I was pushing things.

"Where's that boy with the horse?" I heard the large man say. Clearly I had turned invisible again. I was right here . . . exactly where he had seen me last. He could have looked just a foot or two to the right but he was too busy complaining that I hadn't done the job yet.

"If I give you a byline, son," said Mr. Clark, lowering his voice though no one was listening to us in the first place, "I can't guarantee publication. You're still green, you're still learning the trade."

"I understand, Mr. Clark. But I just want the chance to prove myself. I don't expect any favors."

"Like getting a byline?"

I couldn't help but grin, and it was okay because Mr. Clark had this little smile curling the edge of his lips. Almost imperceptible, but you noticed things like that when you were someone like me.

"Hey, now, that's just good business. We're just making a deal."

"Just making a deal. Well, Brant, I can't believe I'm agreeing to this. But, yes, let's find you a name and get you that byline."

"Thank you, sir. You won't regret it."

"I already do." His smile grew just a bit wider. "Now you'd better get that horse to that girl, because I'm freezing my rear end out here."

"I think I've found the subject of my first article," I joked.

"Brant!"

I laughed and held up my hands. "Okay, okay . . ." I turned and made my way back to the staging area. I didn't actually know where this horse was hiding, but figured it was as good a place as any to start.

Sure enough I found it, standing in a small makeshift shelter being cared for by an old hunched man who reminded me an awful lot of Mr. Doyle from my neighborhood. I walked up to him.

"Hey, so I have to take the horse to the girl," I said.

The old man looked at me with deep suspicion.

"So . . . What do I do here, are there any reins or a rope or anything?" I looked at the horse, even though I'd been avoiding it until now. Man, that animal looked huge this close up.

Now I wasn't exactly what you'd call scared of horses.

Maybe it was more they were scared of me. After all, how else could you explain being tossed off every single one you'd ever tried to ride? Made me happy to live in a time when most folks drove cars.

"Reins get in the way. Just take her by the bridle. She's docile enough. Good little lady," replied the old man.

Little? Hardly.

"So I just . . ." I didn't know what to say. I stared at the beast. She was beautiful, a rich chestnut brown with a white star in the middle of her forehead. But she was still . . . a beast.

"The bridle, just grab fast and lead her."

"And . . . you can't do this because?"

The old man scoffed. "Look at me, son. Those folks don't want me out there in public. Besides. I'm not too well fond of heights."

Well, I'm not too well fond of horses, I thought, but I didn't say it.

"You'd better get going. I'm not getting in trouble because you're scared of horses."

"I'm not!" I said a little too quickly.

"Her name's Trix. She'll follow you."

"Hi there, Trix," I said, trying to calm my nerves. The horse didn't seem to acknowledge my existence. What else was new? I reached up and gently gripped the bridle. My knuckles brushed against her fur, and I flinched slightly in anticipation of her anger but she did nothing. Just stood there, patiently. "Good girl," I said, my heart in my throat. Man, this was embarrassing feeling this way. Just deal with it, Brant. Be a grown-up, for crying out loud.

I wasn't sure what to do next so I just started to walk toward the platform. Sure enough, as the old man had said, Trix followed me. Walked right next to me, those giant hooves clicking on the metallic stage as we approached the stairs to the platform.

"About time," I heard someone say as we materialized around the corner. I didn't look in their direction. I was too focused on not being trampled to death.

The stairs up to the diving platform loomed in front of me. They were raked on a low angle, obviously to allow a horse to climb them. They were shallow too, making the whole thing appear ramp-like. It also had the effect of making the girl at the top appear even farther away. Why was I doing this and why did it seem like this task would never end?

I guided Trix onto the first step and she took it easily. I felt her gently pull as she clearly realized what was what. Whether she saw her rider at the top, the brunette in the bathing suit probably freezing to death in this weather but looking as serene as any bathing beauty on the beach, or whether she was excited to do the dive (which made no sense to me at all), I didn't know, but she wanted to get to the top. So I sped up my walk and decided to just keep my gaze forward and up and not at the horse or at the ground as it was falling away from us.

The platform shook as we walked, oh that was fun. The girl turned and noticed us then. I averted my gaze. I didn't think she wanted some guy just staring at her the way I knew I was. It wasn't about her, of course, I just needed to stare at something, but it probably came across as impolite. I looked instead at her feet. They were bare. How was she not completely frozen through?

"Hi there!" she said suddenly.

It took me by surprise. I had been so focused and was not expecting any conversation at the moment.

"Hi," I replied. I smiled because I didn't want her to think I was scared about all this. The shame burned inside me. If she wasn't scared and she was about to sit on this giant animal and step out into the sky riding it, well . . . I at least could pretend to be at ease.

"Thank you for doing this. I'm guessing Steve didn't show up?" she said.

I had no idea who Steve was. Was she making small talk? Up here? In the sky?

"I don't know," I replied. "But they needed someone to help out." I felt myself step backward even as Trix moved her head to pull me forward.

"I'm like that!" she said.

"Like what?" I was more confused now than ever.

"Oh, just, when someone needs help, I help. I was meaning to say I appreciate it that you helped. That is, I understand why you volunteered."

Why was she still talking? I just wanted her to take the bridle already. This was not a job I had volunteered for, lady.

"Okay," I said. I glanced down again, looking at the small crowd gathered around the base of the platform. Was something actually broken? Was the thing about to collapse? "Look, I need to get back down, so do you need help up?"

"Ha, back down, help up," she said.

Now it sounded like she was speaking in riddles. What was it about performers and their personalities? "Well, do you?"

"Oh, yes. Yes, I do."

Great. I had kind of hoped she was going to say no. But I offered. Because that's what a gentleman does. Right, Uncle?

"So . . . what do I do?" I had a moment of absolute fear that she needed me to lift her onto the horse. Holding a half-naked girl was not something I was prepared to do.

"Oh, just hold her steady while I get on. She's a good little lady, she'll be easygoing though."

Yeah, that's what the old man had said too. Not that he'd been proven wrong yet. But horses could surprise you. I just nodded.

"Need any help?" called out the large man just then. He didn't sound actually worried or like he was sincerely offering or anything. Likely because he wasn't. He was ordering us both to just get on with it.

"I guess we should get on with it," said the girl.

She understood too, obviously. "I guess."

I held on tight as the girl seemed to defy gravity and jumped up on Trix's back. For her part, Trix barely moved, was steady as a rock. My presence was probably not needed at all. I glanced up and watched as the girl settled herself into her position.

"You all set?" I asked.

"Oh yes!" she replied, looking down at me with a charming smile. "Yes, thank you so much."

Okay, so . . . now what? "I'll go then?"

"Yes, please!" she replied. Her voice was a little tight; maybe she was nervous too. Maybe I was making things more complicated for her by still being up here. I quickly released the bridle and turned to make my way down the steps. They suddenly looked very steep and very long.

"My name is Constance, by the way," she called out after me.

I turned around to look at her. "I know," I said. And I turned back to tackle the stairs.

It wasn't until I reached the bottom that I realized what I'd said.

I hadn't known her name. Why had I said it like that? And why hadn't I introduced myself to her as she clearly expected?

It was my dumb stupid pride. I worked hard to hide it. I needed to. I wasn't going to get anywhere being a proud son of a gun. But sometimes it just peeked out from its hiding spot. "I know." I wasn't some stupid invisible kid who had no clue what he was doing or who anyone in this crowd of fancy people was. I knew things.

There it was again, that tinge of shame at my behavior. It always followed me everywhere. Even when I felt so sure of myself, it was always there to remind me after the fact. Never stopped me from doing the thing in the first place. No, that would be too helpful.

I turned just in time to watch the girl fly through the air on Trix and land with a large splash in the small pool.

Now that was bravery.

Or stupidity.

Not much difference between them really, when you thought about it.

Fear.

Anger.

Shame.

All a whirlwind now. All one thing now. A feeling that is not. An existence that is not. And yet we are here.

And yet we feel.

Isn't it strange to not exist and yet to be real?

Seasick. Fantastic. This is why I hated boats. It was pretty straight-forward. You get on a boat, it rocks, you feel like crap. End of story. See, I always had a reason why I thought what I think. There was always an explanation.

But you try to explain to Ally why you took back your job. After you were fired. After they stole your life's work from you. You try to explain that to her. She just didn't get it and that infuriated me. There wasn't any reason she shouldn't understand. She's the one who stayed anyway, who worked with that man still, so why was it that bad if I was the one who said yes? Yes, I'll have my job back. Yes, I'll fix the machine. Yes, I'll get it out of the studio, out of the way of prying eyes and a far too curious writer girl at the studio. Yes, I'll go back to a job that never seemed to give a fig about me. About what I did.

What did I do?

What *did* I do.

You know, at my age I was just a bit too old for comic books, but I do once in a while glance at *Superman*. Heroes that could just save the day made me happy. It was so easy for them. The line between right and wrong was obvious. I wished real life was that obvious. What's good, what's bad, clear and easy.

I know what we did.

I know what we made.

But it's also an invention unlike anything before it. You just can't abandon something like that. Not when you were so close. You don't abandon a kid because they break a few glasses. Because they cry out and smack you across the face by mistake.

A kid just needs help to grow up. You don't abandon your child.

It's not just a machine, it's a miracle.

You don't abandon a miracle.

Even if it scares you.

Even if it kills you.

4: CONSTANCE

"Thank you, thank you, thank you!"

I smiled as Molly squeezed the air out of me. I really hoped whatever she had wasn't catching, but I wasn't about to tell her not to hug me. Can't hurt the poor girl's feelings.

"You're welcome," I wheezed instead.

She backed off with a smile and held my hands in hers. The look of gratitude on her face was sweet and ridiculous. Both my sisters tended to act like they were performing in front of an audience at all times. But at least with Molly there was some kind of sincerity to it.

"I swear you'll never have to do that again," she said. She sneezed into her hanky, releasing one of my hands but yanking my other to follow her. I allowed myself to be pulled toward her and Lily's bedroom. Originally I had shared with Lily, but she got so frustrated by my "silly science experiments," as she called them, that Molly had graciously offered to switch rooms with me. Oh, to be as sweet as Molly. Oh, I knew many people thought I was, but that's not the real me. I'm always frustrated or on edge. Molly's intentions were pure kindness.

"It was okay," I replied. "It's been a long time since I dove. Trix was a dear."

"Isn't she just a darling?" asked Molly as she threw open the door to their room. "Ta-da!"

It took a moment for me to see it among the faded florals that decorated their room. Clothes were everywhere, as usual, on Lily's bed, and my eyes were always drawn to the mess. I didn't even notice the blue flat box on Molly's.

Until I did.

"Molly . . . you didn't," I said, releasing her hand and slowly walking toward her bed.

"I did!" She was positively giddy and clapped her hands together like a child. And then froze. And sneezed loudly.

I floated toward the box and read the words that I knew were printed on it with that picture of the creepy little boy holding the vial: "Gilbert Chemistry Outfit."

"You got me the Master Chemistry Set?" I asked in awe, scared to open the thing.

"Yes! I know you didn't want to dive, and I know you hate being the center of attention, you shy little thing, and I just knew you wanted it. I mean, how could I not! You couldn't stop staring at it every time we passed old Doc's store." She continued on like that, telling my own life story back to me as if it was new to me. I just placed the box back on the bed and carefully opened it.

Inside were several dozen small bottles with bright orange labels, each detailing their contents. There were vials with strange powders, and a scale and a magnet and a book with experiments to try. I felt tears welling up, and I turned to Molly, who was still regaling me with her tale of magnificence, and grabbed her and squeezed her hard.

That shut her up.

"Oh," she said, startled. She hugged me back.

"This is the best gift anyone has ever given me," I said softly. "Thank you, Molly."

We broke apart and I think she could see the tears then because she was flustered and had gone a little red.

"Well, as I said, I know that it was a big thing for you to do what you did today."

"It's so expensive" was all I could say back.

"Don't think about that," she replied.

I looked at her carefully. "Molly, where did you get the money?"

She sighed and shook her head.

"Did someone buy this for you?" I asked.

Another sigh.

"Molly!"

"I know how you feel about men buying me presents, but I promise I'm a big girl and besides, I like presents. Especially if they are for my sisters," she said with that soft, sweet smile of hers. Everything about her appearance was soft and gentle. A round face, soft curves of her body, curly hair that never quite stayed in place. So much softness for someone who was such an athlete.

"I worry" was all I could say. I wanted to say so much more. I wanted to shake her and tell her that these men were not worth her time. That they all were creeps and she was so much better than them. That they only wanted this soft illusion she put out into the world, not the real, funny, generous girl she was. That I worried about her reputation. Not that I personally thought how others did, but I knew how others saw her and Lily. It was unfair and made me extremely frustrated that the boys who courted my sisters didn't have the exact same reputation concerns. They could get away with a lot more than us girls. Yet it was what it was. And I didn't want people thinking negative things about my lovely Molly.

But I couldn't say these things. I never could. I kept all such messy thoughts to myself. How could I say these things knowing how upset she'd get? She was so pleased to have got me this gift.

"I'm fine," Molly said, and I was saved from blurting out something I'd maybe regret by Lily bursting into the room.

"Constance! Come on, we're going to be late!"

I glanced at Molly and we shared a look, *that* look, *our* look that meant, "Oh, Lily."

My sixteen-year-old little sister was a whirlwind at the best of times, but before a show she was a tornado. There was nothing anyone could do but just follow the path of destruction and try to put things back in order in its wake.

"I'm coming," I said. My hair was still damp and I knew I looked a fright, but I told myself it wouldn't really matter, I would be backstage. Besides, Lily probably liked that I looked like some kind of drowned rat. Not that she was an unkind person. She just liked being the center of attention. A lot.

I looked one last time at Molly, who had sat down on her bed and was now blowing her nose daintily. It was quite impressive that she could be so dainty and disgusting at the same time. "Thank you again," I said.

"Connnnnnnstaaaaance!" It was both a whine and a yell coming from the front door.

"You'd better go," replied Molly.

I laughed and went to join Lily, who was already holding my gray wool coat outstretched for me. I grabbed it and put it on, cinching the belt tightly at my waist.

"No hat?" she asked as we stepped out onto the landing and I closed the door behind us.

"You want me to take the time to pin it on?" I asked, reaching into my pockets to grab my gloves.

"No," she replied with a pout, adjusting her own cloche hat on her head.

Lily had such a silly sense of propriety even as others gave her the side eye for dancing in such revealing costumes at the show.

We were met with a cold gust of wind as we stepped onto the street and turned left toward the Boardwalk. Lily was walking at a pace that if she went any faster, we'd be jogging.

I tried my best to keep up with her but fell behind slightly. I wanted to tell her to slow down, we weren't late, everything was fine, but I didn't want to start an argument.

So I walked there, behind her, thinking about the day I'd already had. Of the dive into the freezing water. In front of such a crowd, and caught on film forever. I hoped I had looked professional and confident. I hoped I'd looked pretty. No, don't think like that. There was more to life than looking pretty. Sometimes it's hard when your older sister is famous for flying through the sky on a horse, and your younger sister dances in sequins and feathers, not to wonder, just a little bit . . . and care. I mindlessly touched the top of my head, still wet. And if the air got any colder, I might end up wearing a helmet of ice.

I should have worn a hat.

We arrived at the Boardwalk and the winds picked up. The waves were crashing against the empty beach below and I was grateful we'd done the dive when we had. The weather was churning itself up into a dangerous frenzy now.

It was amazing that there were any tourists at all wandering the Boardwalk, but there were. They came all year round, though in much smaller numbers now. Possibly "tourist" was the wrong word for these kinds of people. In the off-season, it seemed that the people who came to Atlantic City did it for business reasons. Or for other, more illicit ones. They weren't here to see the sights, they were here to escape into the nightclubs or expensive restaurants. Hole themselves up in suites on the top floors of the fanciest hotels.

Speaking of . . . we entered the Oceanview Hotel and rushed through the lobby toward the theater doors of the Diamond Lounge. "Thank you, Jack!" I called out behind me to the doorman, who touched the tip of his hat in return.

We flew through the theater doors. The houselights were up, making the magic of the space disappear into the dark corners, and the blandness of the room was brought into stark relief: the stains on the carpet, the peeling wallpaper, the scratches and notches on the furniture.

"There you are," said Mac, the stage manager. He was adjusting the legs of the curtain stage right, one of his huge cigars dangling out of the corner of his mouth.

"Be careful, Mac, you might light the place on fire," said Lily with her lilting laugh.

"Never have before," he replied with a grin.

"Hey, Mac," I said as Lily raced past him toward backstage.

"Hey there, kiddo," he replied. "What's new with the great scientist?"

I shook my head. It was so embarrassing that he called me that. Ever since he found out I was keen on chemistry, he thought I was some kind of scientist or something. Which I really wasn't. Not one bit. But of course he enjoyed calling me that and I didn't want to upset him by asking him not to.

"Speaking of which," I said instead, "Molly got me the chemistry set."

"Did she now? Well, isn't that just such a nice thing for a sister to do."

"It really is. I was thinking, maybe I could figure out some of those fog effects you were looking for," I replied. My stomach got all fluttery at the thought.

"Now that would be excellent. You do that, and we'll pay you for the privilege, don't you worry!" Mac was always so enthusiastic about everything, it was sometimes hard to tell if he was being sincere. But he was. He was just that lovely.

I smiled and he looked over his shoulder and back at me again.

"You'd better get back there. It's chaos already."

"Really? It's just a Tuesday night show."

"Chaos doesn't care what day of the week it is," he replied, taking a puff of his cigar.

I didn't really understand his point, but I smiled and quickly made my way backstage. Rows of mirrors framed with lights were engaged with rows of girls sitting in front of them, poking and prodding at their faces, adding color and highlights. Other girls stood pulling up stockings and throwing their street clothes over chairs while rushing to grab their costumes off the rack. There definitely was a chaotic energy as the girls got ready for the show. I was their dresser, assistant, whatever they needed to make sure they got onstage on cue and looked fabulous. Sometimes buttons needed to be sewn on, sometimes headpieces needed more hairpins, that sort of thing. It was a relatively easy job when the girls weren't in a fluster. Like they were today.

"Constance! Help!" A bedazzled Naomi jumped in front of

me and presented her back. With my gloves still on, I did up her buttons and she flew away back to her mirror the moment my fingers released her.

I quickly peeled off my coat and gloves and tossed them on one of the few empty chairs, when I was accosted by three girls talking a mile a minute and over one another. I nodded at their requests, not fully understanding them and feeling overwhelmed by the energy and panic.

This was definitely turning out to be one of *those* days.

5: BRANT

"Brant, not now." Mr. Clark sat down heavily behind his desk and took off his hat. He rubbed his bald head a few times, like he was about to make a wish.

"Yes, now, Mr. Clark," I said. Bravery or stupidity, didn't matter.

"It's been a long morning with that stupid horse thing," he said.

"Yes, I know, but you also promised me a byline if I was a stupid horse helper, and I have a doozy of an idea." I sat in the chair opposite him without being asked to. I was feeling pretty invincible, to tell the truth.

"Pitch me fast," said Mr. Clark.

I nodded and scooted to the edge of my seat. My arms rose up and my hands started moving in the air as I spoke. Yeah, I was an energetic speaker. Broke some stuff as a kid in the apartment, got in trouble. And did it again. Over and over. Last week in fact.

"That rich kid and his dad," I said. "The ones making the tourist film today."

"Yes, that rich kid and his dad. Otherwise known as William and Emmett Chambers. The latter being the man who owns half of Atlantic City."

"Well, that's my point. How about an exposé on the corruption in Atlantic City, with Mr. Chambers at the center of it?" Sounded pretty swell to me.

"How about that," replied Mr. Clark, decidedly not that enthused.

"It's a solid story," I said.

"It's an old story, it's a known story. You telling me there's corruption in Atlantic City? The home of probably more defunct speakeasies than New York? The city that Prohibition made rich? Wow, Brant, I had no idea." Mr. Clark looked at me with an exhausted expression, a world-weary sigh escaping his lips. "You youngsters are all the same. Pitching old stories as new, because you never read the old stuff. You can't ignore history, son. And no one's interested in corruption anymore. Not after the war. They just want to live their lives, however they're funded. You get me?"

Oh, I got him all right. I shook my head; it wasn't fair. "You mean in the same way this paper is funded."

Mr. Clark didn't get angry at that. He just stared blankly at me for a moment and said, "Yup."

Right, I had to think quick. I didn't have any other pitches but this one, and I knew it was a good one. I just had to convince Mr. Clark I was right. "Okay, look, it's old news. But what if I could offer a new perspective?"

"Brant, I really need a quiet moment on my own here . . ."

"The rich kid, the one at the horse diving this morning. William, you said his name was. What about him?"

"Just tell me your idea. These questions are giving me a headache." He pinched the bridge of his nose as he said it in case I didn't believe him. But I did. There were very few things that didn't give Mr. Clark a headache.

"You could tell that he and his father don't exactly get on, that it isn't all hunky-dory there. I bet befriending his son could lead to some pretty interesting information."

Mr. Clark sighed and leaned back in his chair. He swiveled around so his back was to me and he was looking out his unwashed windows, caked with layers of dirt and salt from the sea.

"Look," he said after another sigh. "Write the story you want to write. If it's good, it'll go in the paper. At this point, Brant, I know better than to try to tell you no. But just because I promised you a byline doesn't mean I publish anything that crosses my desk. Still got to be good. Or at least, not embarrassing to the paper."

That was enough for me.

"That's real swell of you, Mr. Clark, real swell. I won't let you down, I promise! I already have a lead! It's a party, a killer-diller of a party, Mr. Clark. Looks like some toughs from New

York are coming up to meet with Mr. Chambers and he wants to show them a good time. I've got a friend who has an in . . ."

"Enough!" interrupted Mr. Clark. "Get out of my office, Brant."

Didn't need to be told more than once. "Sure thing, Mr. Clark! And thank you, Mr. Clark!"

I was excited. This was it! Finally I was getting my chance to prove that I could do more than deliver the mail. You've got to make them see you, no one else is going to do that for you. Another lesson from my uncle. I was darn tired of being invisible; it was time to be noticed.

The dining room was a shining

bright space. So unlike its character from this morning. I leaned against the doorframe to the butler's pantry and stared at the delicate crystal glasses, the facets each with their own little glint dancing around their faces. At the silverware newly polished, the fine china, the candles lit in their silver holders. The lights in the chandelier above bright and welcoming.

And I thought to myself, *This room was not made for the people who live here. This room was made for the people who visit.*

How pathetic.

"You ready, son?"

My father had a way of bursting into a room like the infamous bull in a china shop. The glasses on the table positively shook with fear. I sighed. Of course he was ready. When was I never not ready?

"Yes, Father," I replied.

"Good. How does it look? Does it look expensive?" Father

asked, walking to the table and examining it closely. He found an invisible spot on a knife and spat on it, giving it a rub then with the sleeve of his perfectly tailored suit jacket.

"Father, you can't do that," I said. I motioned to one of the servants who had just placed a giant floral arrangement on the sideboard. He nodded immediately and swooped in, somehow very politely taking the knife from my father's meaty grasp.

"It looks expensive though," he said, turning to me. All day it had been nothing but question after question. My father was trying to make sure everything was perfect for fear of what others might think. I really wished Mother were still alive for moments like these. She'd had a magical calming effect on him. On all of us. She put things into perspective.

Neither Father nor I was particularly good at putting things into perspective.

"Yes, it does," I replied.

"Fancy, right?" He turned back to the table and put his hands on his hips. He seemed pleased.

"Very fancy."

He turned and grinned at me. "You know, the way New York likes it."

"Just that way."

It was never names, with them. With any of them. It was always places. New York. Chicago. Philadelphia. These men self-identified so hard with their cities, it was as if they had built them from the ground up. Ironic since most of them had come to America not so long ago. All of us were newcomers in a way. And if we didn't think it, then we were reminded of it by others. The others who didn't call themselves by city names, but by their own last names. Last names that were meant to suggest a more deeply rooted permanence than cities themselves. Old money.

All of it was for show.

All of it was exhausting.

I didn't want any part of it. Yet here I was. Suddenly. Sitting at a table with a dozen or so men just like my father. Loud, hungry for something more than just the steak at the table, and rich. So very rich.

I'd played this part, attended so many of these dinners, that I didn't even notice how we went from moment to moment, how I ended up eating a bloody steak when I had only just been standing watching my father spit on a knife.

Soon dessert would happen. Had happened.

Then expensive whiskey or brandy for my father and his guests.

Oh, that had happened, too.

Then what?

Then suddenly I'd be standing in some nightclub on the Boardwalk or at an elegant bar in a hotel. Surrounded by noise and uncontrolled laughter. That messy drunken behavior that wasn't quite dangerous enough to break out into fights, but not so safe as to offer a teasing joke without causing deep offense.

Now it wasn't a future possibility. Now I was there. At the Rose Club. The Rose Club? That was a fancy joint. Father had really pulled out all the stops with this visit. In my very sober state, I realized only then that this visit was a big deal for my father. As in, an actual big deal. My father only brought guests to this club if he was engaged in a deal that would have a huge effect on his income and, more importantly, his power in Atlantic City.

I hadn't been paying any attention. Now I regretted it. I was adrift. And I had no idea what was going on. This happened to me sometimes, time slipped in and out. I remember trying to explain to Father as a child this feeling of losing moments. He couldn't grasp the concept and had no desire to try harder. Mother had just died and he hardly had room for his own thoughts. I didn't blame him. But if he'd understood, I'd felt back then, then maybe this could help him too. Help him skip past the scary things, the frustrating things, and just focus on what needed to be done.

It was scary after Mother died. What do we do now without her? How do we live our lives without her support?

Best to ignore those questions.

My life returned to a more regular pace and I was brought back to reality as I was handed a glass of champagne.

"He's seventeen!" a man with a thick New York accent laughed, not really concerned for my moral character, just enjoying the moment.

"Champagne doesn't count!" giggled his date, a short, freckled redheaded woman with a gummy smile.

"It's Atlantic City. Nothing ever counts here," added another fellow.

"Except Emmett's take," said New York–accent man.

They all laughed heartily at my father's greed and clinked glasses. I didn't join them, just placed my full champagne glass on a passing waiter's tray, turned around, and stared at the large dance floor. Swirls of colors slid across my view as folks danced, the band on the bandstand behind. It was amazing that despite the tourist season being long behind us, there were still enough people to fill this room. Still enough folks who needed a drink and a laugh and a spin on the dance floor. Who needed to escape.

What were they running from tonight? What would weigh them down tomorrow morning? Did they see their futures all laid out before them by someone else; did they wish they could turn onto the dirt path and have an adventure or two? Were they trapped?

Were they like me?

And then all the lights went out.

7: CONSTANCE

"You are coming out with us!"

announced Chloe, practically ripping her costume off and kicking it to one side. She took in a deep breath and I didn't blame her; the corsets on the last costume of the night were very tight. I would know. I'd had to tie them.

I shook my head and said, "No, thank you." I really couldn't go out tonight, not after the very long day I'd had. And it was just a Tuesday after all. Why was everyone making a Tuesday so dramatic today?

Chloe grabbed my hand and practically yanked my shoulder out of its socket pulling me toward her. "Makeover time!"

No, please, no. Not makeover time. I hated makeover time.

I was pushed unceremoniously into a chair in front of one of the mirrors. I looked a fright, it was true, and I did enjoy looking presentable, but I hated being dressed up like some doll. This happened every few months, and I had really no idea what was wrong with my normal appearance. I looked over at Lily sitting in front of her mirror. She was already dressed in her regular clothes and was carefully reapplying her going-out makeup after having removed her performance makeup. She looked at me in the mirror and shrugged. Lily was never going to be my savior.

The girls knew I didn't fight back; I never did. They enjoyed it too much and I didn't want to make a fuss no matter how much I disliked their poking and prodding. And of course the underlying message of, "How you look isn't quite good enough." I was quickly turned into their version of Cinderella at the ball, dark eyeliner, bold lipstick, even some rouge. And was passed over to Mirabel, who handed me a black dress with a satin sheen.

"Come on, hurry up," she ordered.

So I hurried.

I stared at myself as I pulled on the dress. I didn't look bad at all. I never had any issue with the end result. But I didn't look like me. I liked my makeup a certain way, a little softer. My clothes a little less showy. It wasn't that I didn't mind looking good, I just thought I already did. Except for today, that is. Today I had been a complete disaster.

Maybe the makeover was warranted. This one time.

"Let's go, let's go!" Ah, there was Lily's familiar insistent whine. The order was followed and soon all of us, including a very exhausted me, were sweeping out of the hotel and onto the Boardwalk in peals of ringing laughter.

Chloe linked her arm in mine and gave me a wink. "You're a good sport," she said. I always liked her. She had the reputation of a typical fiery redhead, but to me she seemed the most down-to-earth of any of the girls in the chorus.

"I'm a pushover," I replied. I was able to be a bit more honest with her than with most.

"You should work on that," she replied.

I nodded. She was right, but I didn't know where to start. I couldn't get past the notion that it was best to keep it all inside. My sisters could be outgoing and share everything they thought and felt because it was safe to. Molly was so lovely through and through, and Lily was harmless and silly even in her demanding ways, but the real me? The inside me? I was certain no one wanted to see that. To see my frustration. To see what I really thought of the world and those in it. No one would understand. It wouldn't work.

To thine own self be true. Shakespeare wrote that. But Shakespeare hadn't been a girl.

We turned down the street, following behind the others and toward a red flashing sign that read "The Rose Club." It might have looked like a dive from the outside, but it was one of the higher-end clubs in Atlantic City and expensive.

"Don't worry," said Chloe as we walked down the short flight of steps to the entrance. "Some swell is paying for all us girls. Silly fellow."

Silly indeed if he thought paying for these girls meant he'd get anything special in return. They weren't stupid, these ladies. They knew how to handle these kinds of guys. You could almost feel sorry for them, the way they fawned and spent lavishly with such high unmet hopes. But . . . not really.

All I could do was nod. I hated being paid for by anyone, even people with good intentions. I liked not having to rely on anyone. Maybe it was seeing Molly and Lily receive so many gifts over the years, but I didn't want that. I wanted to be self-sufficient.

We checked our coats and were met then by a wall of noise and swirls of color. The place was packed. But like a school of fish, our group maneuvered together and managed to acquire a corner table onto which purses and gloves exploded in a colorful mess.

"Do you want a drink?" asked Chloe.

"Oh," I replied, feeling appropriately overwhelmed. "I guess a soda pop."

Chloe laughed. "I'm going to get you a real drink."

I meant to tell her that I was too young and honestly not particularly interested in alcohol, but she held up her finger and looked at me intently. So I didn't say anything and she quickly vanished into the crowd.

I felt suddenly alone. It was interesting really, when you thought about it. Here I was surrounded by so many people and yet I could go for a walk by myself along the Boardwalk and feel perfectly content. Normally I would be happy just to observe—this was not my first party, nor my first time at a nightclub. I liked watching people, I enjoyed seeing happy faces and watching them laugh and dance together. I liked when life was colorful and pretty. When, just for a little while, cares and worries were set aside.

But today felt so different. All day something had been tickling my spine.

I shook my head. It had to have been the dive this morning. I could still feel the wind against my face; feel my stomach turn over, looking down at the water far below me. The inky blackness. Suddenly all I wanted to do was go home and go to bed and wake up refreshed with a new day of possibilities in front of me.

My unfocused gaze landed on a familiar face. The rich kid from earlier. The one I'd seen darting about around the base of the diving platform. He was standing with a group of large boisterous men, the kind of men who always laughed just a little too loudly at parties, who never quite finished their drinks but always refilled their glasses. The rich kid looked miserable. My heart went out to him then. We all have our own problems; it's all relative. Even those who live in palaces have days where the walls feel like they are caving in, I assumed. I mean, we are all human after all.

I was watching the rich kid closely now, wondering about him, who he really was, why his father needed to shoot that film of his, when I noticed a different young man walking toward me suddenly. He crossed into the path between me and the rich kid and smiled as he did. He was quite handsome, I observed, dark hair parted neatly, a perfectly cut suit. A dimple in one cheek.

It didn't occur to me that he was walking toward me until he started talking and said, "Eyes meeting across a crowded room."

I stared at him. He seemed suddenly very close. Like he had just materialized right in front of me then, hand outstretched.

"What?" I said. It was the wrong thing to say, but when did I ever manage to say the right thing?

The young man laughed. "I saw you looking at me. I must say, I've never been more flattered."

I just stared at him, at his deep brown eyes, the slight crinkle at the edges. He was amused by me. Oh, how I disliked amusing people like this. People either thought I was rude or amusing. I was always an object of some kind of fascination. All because I couldn't quite say the words I wanted to the way one ought to. Yet another reason to just keep everything to myself. No one seemed to understand me. More than that, no one tried to understand me.

"Oh well," I said, utterly confused. And then, it hit me. Somehow this man had thought my staring was directed at him. Now my cheeks were definitely burning. Thank goodness the room was overly warm and he wouldn't notice.

"I'm Andrew," he said. I realized his outstretched hand was meant for me to take and I grabbed it awkwardly. He gave my hand a little shake and then released it.

I looked at him some more. Truly he was very good-looking. Tall. Slender but strong. There was something also very pleasing about his presence, almost calming.

"And . . ."

And? "And?"

He laughed and I no longer felt particularly calm. What was I missing?

"Your name is?" he asked.

Of course! I wasn't stupid, I knew how introductions worked. "Oh, yes, of course, I'm Constance."

"It's nice to meet you," replied Andrew.

Now I was starting to slowly feel frustrated. He spoke with expectations in his voice and stood there silently as if I was supposed to read his mind. But I honestly was rather confused. I didn't generally get approached by anyone in these situations. Why now?

Then I remembered the dress. And the makeup. And the hair.

And oh, my goodness, he thought I was staring at him before.

This is a boy-girl thing happening now, isn't it? I asked myself. *You aren't a child; you can do this.* It wasn't as if I'd never been on an outing with a boy before, or even kissed one. Once. That one time. Oh, how Lily would laugh at me now with my chaste little ways, as she called them. Where was she?

"Nice to meet you too." Though was it? Was it maybe too stressful really? Why did I suddenly miss feeling so very alone? How was it I now missed that strange dread in my soul and the memory of the cold-water dive? Were those feelings better than the flustered confusion I was feeling now? I think yes. At least I understood the former. The latter was so out of my control.

"Care to dance?"

Not really.

"Yes, that would be lovely."

So that happened. He took my hand gently and I noticed this time how soft and warm it was. I also noticed how clammy and cold mine were. How he must regret doing this. But he didn't seem to. He escorted me to the dance floor and then the other hand was on my waist. That didn't help my flustered feelings. But I focused on the music and on the dance steps. I wasn't a bad dancer after all. We all were quite good at such things, the Gray sisters. Even the one who refused to go into show business, who was happy behind the scenes. Even she, that is to say, even I, enjoyed a good turn about the room.

And good it was. He was very elegant, and sure-footed. He had grace. He was no Fred Astaire, but who in real life was?

I started to feel dizzy.

"If you look at me, it will help," he said, clearly noticing.

Well, that was a problem now, wasn't it? I was purposefully trying not to look at him. Looking at him made me feel very vulnerable. Because I rather liked looking at him.

I looked at him. He smiled. I smiled.

Maybe it's okay to feel flustered sometimes. Maybe it's a good feeling. Maybe it's a really good feeling.

I felt myself settle into his arms. Not quite relaxed, but not not. It was nice.

And then everything went black.

8: BRANT

"This isn't what I had in mind when you said you'd get me into the party," I said under my breath.

"Shh," replied Mike.

I shook my head as I stood there listening to the maître d' give us instructions on the proper way to pass around drinks and food.

"Circulate, always circulate," he said in a thick French accent that sounded almost too French.

"If that guy's French, then I'm a goldfish," I muttered.

"I said shh!"

The maître d' gave us a stern look. "Something wrong, Monsieur Michael?"

"No, sir," replied Mike, taking in a sharp inhale of breath. I snorted at that.

"You have your instructions, now *allez!*" said the maître d' with a clap of his hands.

We were hustled over to a staging area. As I picked up a

tray, I said, "I thought we were going to the party, not working the party."

Mike rolled his eyes at me. "I said I'd get you in, and you're in. Stop being such a drip."

I could have said something then about how Mike was so much of a drip that he was soaking wet. But I refrained and instead just took the tray with the little cheese puffs on it because I knew for a fact if I took the one with the champagne flutes that it would all be on the floor before I even made it out to the guests.

We left the small kitchen and entered the glittering party room, complete with a dance floor and band playing. Looked like a swell party. Would have been fun to be a guest. Not a darn waiter. I turned to find Mike to chew him out some more, but he'd already vanished into the crowd.

"Circulate, Monsieur Morris." The maître d' drew a circle with his finger as he hissed the instruction in my ear before swanning off to kiss some partygoers on each cheek. Quite a talent really, to do all that in just one motion. Needed good coordination for that. I picked up a cheese puff and popped it into my mouth and decided to make the best of it. So I circulated.

And honestly, it turned out it was in fact a pretty excellent excuse to wander through the crowd looking for William Chambers. I'd never tell Mike that.

"Ooh, puffy cheese!" A tall man with very red cheeks suddenly bent his head into my line of vision to examine each little puff.

"Yeah," I said as I watched him breathe on everything. I made a small note in my mental notepad never to eat anything that's been "circulated" ever again. He eventually picked up a little puff right in the middle of everything, his hand grazing a couple as he went in for the kill.

Then he was off. And I was still watching his long limbs retreat into the crowd when another hand emerged from beside me.

Instinctively I said, "Don't!" Then quickly turned to apologize for the outburst. "I'm very sorry, it's just that . . ." I stopped. I was staring at a bewildered William Chambers. Here he was, right there in front of me. I quickly changed my tone from apologetic to conspiratorial. If there was one thing I knew about people, it's that they loved to think they were in on a secret. I lowered my voice, which automatically made him move in closer to hear me. "There was a fellow just now, touched almost all of them. I wouldn't recommend eating one."

William looked at me, confused, but didn't say much of anything, just sort of nodded. He seemed strangely out of sorts; maybe he was just drunk. But it was different. It spooked me a little. I wrote a note in my brain about it. I'd need to, at some point, transpose everything inside my head onto a real piece of paper. Needed to remind myself to do that.

I watched as William turned to look somewhere else. His mind seemed heavily occupied but I really wanted to knock on its door to see if I was allowed in.

"Are you William Chambers?" I asked. Might as well just go for it, I thought.

And that's when the world went black.

I knew immediately what was going on, though I seemed to be one of the only ones. I guessed these rich folks weren't as used to blackouts as I was. It's why my uncle would always go on and on about the good ol' days when you didn't have to rely on electricity and such. Candles, boy oh boy, did he love candles.

Folks were getting nervous, and you could tell people were moving about, trying to do something useful, trying not to panic. I knew that if the lights didn't get turned on soon things would get a lot more manic, likely even dangerous. A large group of drunk revelers trapped down in a basement club in the dark? Just as I thought it, I found myself on the floor. Someone had crashed into me hard.

"I'm so sorry. Are you all right?"

I didn't know who was talking to me, but I felt a hand on my shoulder and I was helped up.

"We need to get to the fuse box," the voice said. "I can fix this if I get to a fuse box."

"I agree," I replied. "It's in the kitchen, I saw it. Come with me. Follow my voice."

My body remembered the way back, and called out to my new friend to follow. I didn't know if he had been able to in the dark until we made it inside the kitchen. The gas was still working, so the burners of the stove were still on. It was a small amount of light, but it seemed like the sun compared with the pitch black in the ballroom.

I turned to my friend and that's when I realized it was William. I stared at him as he darted past, looking for the fuse box. This kid was going to save the day?

I watched him from a distance, a shadow now, barely an outline, moving about. Trying to find a replacement for the fuse, I guessed. He seemed to know what he was doing. And sure enough, suddenly, the lights were back on.

Just like that.

New tactic, not conspiratorial. Time for familiarity. That might work.

"What does a rich kid like you know about fixing things," I asked, approaching him.

William closed the door containing the fuses, playing with the spent one in his hand. "Have we met before?" he asked, looking confused and a little suspicious of me.

I smiled and stuck out my hand to shake. "Brant Morris. You're William Chambers. I was at the horse-diving event this morning."

William looked at my hand for a moment, and then smiled. He took it. "It's Bill. Nice to meet you, Brant. And I like fixing things, what can I say!"

"Didn't know things needed fixing in your neck of the woods," I said, leaning against the countertop. Staff were flooding into the kitchen now, and the maître d' was already barking orders. But I was determined to have this conversation with William, or rather, Bill.

"Things always need fixing," he said. It sounded deep the way he said it, meaningful. Maybe it was. Or maybe it was just his way. Everything about him seemed confident. This was a man who knew he was meant to take up space in this world. Maybe he just meant that objects break, and you need to fix them.

"Right this way, monsieur." I finally turned toward the chaos as the maître d' came right for us with a man in coveralls behind. As he approached, I saw a stitched-on name tag that had "Scott" written on it, and underneath the word "GENT" spelled out in all capital letters.

"It was just a fuse," said Bill as Scott the Gent gentleman passed him, not even giving him a second glance.

"Nothing 'just' about this system," replied Scott gruffly, opening the metal door and looking inside the small closet-like space.

Bill went over to join him. "Well, I also had to reattach a loose wire here," he said, and pointed.

"You! Get back to work!" The maître d' grabbed me by my shoulder and I whipped around fast at that.

"You better remove that hand there before I snap my cap."

The maître d' backed away slowly, shooting daggers at me, but it wasn't like I was planning on this work arrangement to be any kind of a long-term deal. I was okay with his anger. I had more important things to do. Like get this story.

I turned back in time to see Bill and Scott shaking hands.

"Not a bad job, kid," said Scott. "You ever need a gig, let me know."

"Thank you, sir," replied Bill, and I couldn't help but laugh. Both of them looked at me, confused.

"Oh, come on, like this rich kid needs a gig," I said.

Scott looked at Bill, then back at me. Then he shook his head and picked up his tools, and was on his way, the word "Gent" on the back of his coveralls disappearing behind the cooks and waiters.

I looked at Bill and he was staring at me kind of funny. Shoot. I'd miscalculated. I thought maybe he was the kind of guy who was tired of yes-men, who'd appreciate someone being a down-to-earth son of a gun with him. But of course, now that I thought about it, how many rich folk actually appreciated that? Especially from a complete stranger.

"Hey," I said, making to apologize, "look . . ."

"You want to grab a drink?" asked Bill, interrupting.

Or . . . maybe I was right on the money. Right on a big stinkin' sack of money.

9: CONSTANCE

It isn't that I didn't like people,

it's that I didn't like when there were lots of people. In the same room. At the same time. But what I disliked even more than a large group of people was a large group of people panicking in the pitch black.

My dancing partner was holding me close still, and I discovered I was holding him back, my hands gripping his arms tightly. He didn't seem afraid or concerned. In fact he laughed a little.

"Well now, this is fun," he said. But when I didn't respond, his tone changed. It became softer. "Are you alright?"

There was a crash from across the room, and a scream, and I knew instantly that the crowd was about to turn from a group of nervous individuals to a single entity. Like a droplet on a microscope slide, slipping toward and then becoming one with another. Andrew didn't seem to understand the imminent threat, or if he did, didn't seem to care. I shook my head.

It was time to simply take charge.

I slipped my hand down his arm and took his hand in

mine. "Come on," I said with a giggle. He resisted only for a moment and then allowed me to pull him through the dark. It was something my sisters had taught me. If you want someone to do something for you, ask with a smile or a giggle. I didn't understand why it worked, but it did. I just wanted to ask things normally, but evidently when I asked things normally I was too "severe."

It was surprisingly easy to guide him through to the doors and out into the fresh air. I knew the way well enough, and walking with purpose, even in the dark, is an effective way of getting somewhere even if you are a little lost. Even if you are bumping into drunk dancers and panicking waiters.

"Where are we going?" he asked, but he didn't sound like he cared about the answer. There was a tinge to his voice that made it sound like he thought this whole experience was adorable. I wasn't sure how I felt about that.

I just wanted air and sky and sea. I just wanted to be away from everyone, from the crowd melting out of the club into the street, from my sister. And yet I held on to his hand, so I supposed, as I pulled him toward the Boardwalk, I didn't want to be away from absolutely everyone.

I released his hand as I reached out toward the railing separating the Boardwalk from the sandy drop a few feet below. I grabbed on to it tight and closed my eyes, taking a deep breath, inhaling the salt and the cold air. I felt a sudden intense memory of that morning, of falling through wind, of landing in the water. Of the chaos, the rushing, the kicking and trying to find which way was up. I opened my eyes and felt my legs give way and I crumpled to the ground.

I sat leaning against a post, breathing hard, staring across the Boardwalk at the James' Salt Water Taffy shop, closed and dark. This feeling of dread I'd had all day. Something was wrong.

I shook my head no. That was a lie. Our emotions lie to us. Nothing was wrong. Everything was quite well, as a matter of fact. You got a gift, you went to a party, and then there was a blackout. A very common thing. All is quite well.

"You're a gas!" said the young man, sitting down next to me. He was out of breath and I looked at him. Had I been running? I hadn't thought I had been running. My breath came fast and thin, but that was more about my mind, I thought.

Had I been running?

"Oh well, I just needed some air," I said. I smiled though. He smiled back. He was having a good time and I felt relieved. It didn't matter that in this moment I was feeling strange and out of sorts; he was having a good time and that was something.

Was it though?

"Boy, I'll say." He laughed again and turned his whole body to face me. "This ground is freezing. Are you sure you're okay?"

No, I was definitely not sure of that.

"We should stand up," I said. He gallantly rose and helped me up. It was very nice. I didn't know what to do now that I was standing looking at him so I turned and faced the ocean once more.

"I never get bored of this," I said. There was a waning crescent of a moon that night, like a last farewell of light. Funny to think of it like that now. It reflected on the ocean, on the whitecaps of the waves.

"I can understand why not." He stood next to me so that his arm and mine touched. "Do you live here?"

I nodded. "I do."

"And you're a dancer." I shook my head. He noticed. "You're not?"

I looked at him. "I'm not anything." I felt the return of the strange dark twinge in my gut but I didn't break eye contact.

"That's impossible," he replied with a laugh.

"No, it's very possible." I looked back out to sea and saw then a silhouette on the horizon. Ships came and went with great frequency here, but there was something about this one. Just appearing like that out at night, so late, so secret. I remembered the stories of ships in the '20s bringing alcohol illegally down from Canada. But of course that was over now.

"You are definitely a something. A someone," he quickly corrected. "You're Constance."

I'm Constance. Constant Constance. Yes, that was true. Always reliable, there for any situation. Like some everyday household item, like a pair of gardening gloves.

I looked at Andrew and there was nothing else to say or do so I just smiled. He smiled back. He felt proud, I could tell. He had cheered me up, or so he thought. His work here was done. He looked back out toward the ocean, content in his goodness.

I looked too.

The ship was gone.

I suppose they assumed I was

like my father after all. Even at my age they assumed I'd want to drink alcohol, and, of course, the best kind. Brant's eyes opened so wide that I almost saw the crystal reflected in them.

"No, thank you," I said as the waiter made to pour me a glass. "I'll have a Roy Rogers."

Brant laughed. "Haven't had one of those since I was a kid. Make that two!" He smiled at the waiter, who looked a little confused but nodded and went to get our drinks, leaving the expensive whiskey behind.

Brant stared at it and then laughed again.

"The whole bottle, just like that? If you wanted it?" He shook his head.

The waiter returned almost immediately with our drinks. Service for the son of Emmett Chambers was always top-notch.

"Yes, well," I said, raising my glass, "it's not generosity if you're not paying for it, so don't think anything of it."

"I was impressed. I'm not anymore," he replied. I laughed. "Here's to silver spoons."

"And not choking on them," I replied. We clinked glasses and sipped our drinks. Brant winced a bit at the sweetness.

"I knew places like this existed, but . . ." Brant leaned back in his chair and looked around. He made no effort to look to the manner born. He wasn't, and I liked that he didn't pretend anyway. After all it was a beautiful room. Dark wood paneling, walls of shelves filled with books, a roaring fire for a windy night like tonight. It was also a particularly quiet night, which I liked. A gentleman's club was fine to have as a retreat, but when packed with men drinking the night away and loudly pontificating, it was my idea of, well, the opposite of heaven.

"So," I said, leaning back as well, feeling some of the anxiety from the evening finally melt off my shoulders. "Should I take the job?"

Brant looked at me and rolled his eyes. I laughed again.

"No, but seriously," I said. "Would it be wrong to? I want to learn, and there's only so much you can teach yourself."

"Sometimes we don't have the luxury of teachers," replied Brant.

"I understand." I took another sip. "But when you're offered the chance to be taught, just like that?"

"You could be taking away an opportunity from someone who actually needs it."

I hadn't thought of that. I really hadn't thought of that.

"Then again, maybe you have a special gift, shouldn't waste

that," added Brant, thoughtfully swirling his drink. He was a strange-looking fellow now that I had the time to really appraise him. He was a little short, and a little squat, but not in a way that you'd actually describe him like that. His hair was already receding but he was young—he had to be about my age. Maybe it wasn't that, maybe it was just so thin and light. I wasn't sure what the ladies would make of him, but he had a twinkle in his eye that I bet they enjoyed. I couldn't figure him out but I knew there was something appealing about him and that I appreciated his directness.

"Well, now I have no idea what to do," I replied. And then my stomach sank. "Oh no, no no no no." I slid down into my chair.

"Are you hiding?" asked Brant, turning around in his chair. Darn tootin' I was hiding. "Wait, is that your father?"

Darn tootin' it was my father.

Over the top of Brant's head, there by the entrance having their coats checked by our overly friendly coat-check girl Lola, was my father and the men from New York. The ladies looked to have retired for the night. A pity because now things would turn into late-night festivities much more easily. Maybe even all night.

"Now is that my son I see!" I tried to sink lower into my chair. When my father treated me like an old friend and not like a grave disappointment, nothing good could come from it.

Obviously, I couldn't actually hide from these men. Not in the real world, or in my carefully curated Father-ordained future. They were quickly upon us, dragging heavy chairs painfully noisily across the hardwood floor.

"What have we got here?" asked Mr. Bowman, picking up the decanter, with his very large hand able to wrap almost all the way around it.

"Macallan 18," I replied with a tight-lipped smile.

"It'll do." He snapped for a waiter and, before he made it to our table, called out, "Glasses!"

Father sat down next to me and gave me a look. "Where did you disappear off to?"

"Someone had to get the lights back on," I replied.

He shook his head. "I think they had it under control."

"Actually, sir, thanks to your son, the lights came on a good deal sooner than they would have. We had to wait for the contractor to arrive," said Brant. His tone was polite, far more deferential than when he spoke to me. He knew, then, how to behave around certain people. He knew I was certain people. What made him choose what kind of tone to take?

I glanced at my father and was embarrassed to discover him eyeing Brant with the same expression I found myself sporting. I relaxed my face into a more open one.

"Who's this?" Father asked.

"It's my friend Brant. You've met him before, Father," I said.

Father looked carefully at him, then shrugged. "He does seem familiar."

I didn't think I needed to add that Brant was the one he'd ordered to take the horse up the diving platform. Let him assume he was one of us for now.

"So you fellows up from New York?" asked Brant.

"You can't tell?" I replied, trying to shift the tone.

"New York!" one of the smaller men called out, raising his glass. The others did the same and they drank. Downing their Macallans in one gulp.

"Here on business?" asked Brant.

"What are you, a cop?" asked Mr. Russo with a laugh.

"Why would a cop care if you were here on business?" followed up Brant.

"It's all the questions, not what you're asking," replied my father with an edge to his voice. It wasn't that he didn't like questions; he just preferred to be the one asking them.

Brant definitely heard it and held up a hand in apology. "I'm so sorry, I just get curious."

"Be careful about that," replied my father.

"Well, my uncle always says curiosity is an excellent way to expand your mind," Brant said with a grin.

"Funny, mine said it was a good way to get yourself killed." Father finished his drink and started to pour himself another. "Different strokes for different folks, I guess."

"Very true," replied Brant in his pleasant way.

"Another?" I asked, motioning to the waiter.

Brant nodded with a smile. We exchanged a look. One that

suggested we were in on this together, dealing with the excess of wealth with humor and grace, and not without a great deal of appreciation for the absurdity of it all.

As the waiter replaced his glass, I did have to wonder though, if he wasn't a cop, what was he?

THOMAS CONNOR

I was working with idiots. How hard was it to move something down a flight of stairs? Especially if it was your job to move things. Hire movers, they said. It'll save time, they said.

I pushed the scrawny fellow holding the left side of the crate out of the way and grabbed it myself.

"Come on," I said. Yes it was heavy, but sometimes something heavy felt good. Feeling the strain in your muscles, the work it took, you felt alive. Also sometimes a job just needed to get done. Quit moaning about it.

Moaning.

It hadn't made a peep the whole journey. I wasn't even sure if it was still with us. I didn't understand what was happening and why it had happened yet. I was pretty sure that it was with us though. That it would move with the machine. It had some kind of a connection to it. They all did.

We made it down the first flight of stairs. I pushed the hidden button so we could head down the rest. Scott had found this place, this old factory from Prohibition days. There were lots of places like this in the city, but this one was special. This one had more to it than at first glance.

Glad I had Scott as my right-hand man. Glad he was still around. So many of the Gent men had left Atlantic City by now. Moved to other Gent locations in larger cities with more things that broke and more things to fix. But Atlantic City was our real home. The place where inventions were made. Where the sky filled with light at night, where the Ferris wheel survived harsh icy winds from the ocean. Here we made the special things. The magical things.

Here we had made the machine.

And here we would fix it.

11: CONSTANCE

The next day was bright and cheerful. Almost too bright and cheerful. Possibly it had less to do with the sun sparkling on the water and more to do with Molly's general level of exhausting excitement.

"Tell us everything!" She was squeezing my hand so tight I thought she might pull it right off. Suddenly she released it to quickly fumble for her handkerchief in her pocketbook and sneeze daintily. She was determined to not have a cold even though the cold was not as determined not to have her.

Lily was walking quickly up ahead of us, almost purposefully showing she didn't care, though I didn't know why. We both knew she did. That I came away last night with a beau and she did not was definitely not sitting well with her. Though I'd hardly call the mysterious Andrew my beau.

"There isn't much to tell. We danced and then there was this blackout so we went outside," I replied. "He wants to take me for an early supper tonight before work." As I said it, I realized we were fast approaching that exact same spot he and I had sat on the ground. Lily had wanted some taffy, and though there were many shops that sold it, James was by far the best. That I hadn't made the connection until now just showed me how off I was feeling. Yesterday had been a whirlwind and today I felt utterly spent, exhausted. I looked out to the ocean. It was calmer today, it made me feel better. I knew weather patterns were independent of what emotions we attributed to them, but a calm sea was a kind of balm.

"Isn't that the young man from last night?" asked Lily up ahead. She pointed a gloved finger and I looked, feeling my face get warm and my heart suddenly beating fast.

"Where?" asked Molly with excitement.

Walking toward us wasn't Andrew, but the rich kid.

"You know him?" I asked, but Lily was too far ahead to hear me, or she chose to go back to ignoring me. So I just watched as we moved toward each other. He was in a long tan wool coat, fedora, and gray scarf. He was tall and strong looking, every picture his father. The same chestnut-colored hair too I recalled from the night before though now it was hidden under his hat. A handsome fellow in general, though he didn't seem to under-stand that fact about himself, or, at least, didn't want to be seen to understand it. He looked every bit the role of casual wealth. You saw a lot of it in Atlantic City, turning around corners, walking through doors held open, pointing out to sea and tak-ing photographs, riding by in rickshaws.

There was the trying-too-hard wealth as well, those men who practically carried dollar bills in their fists walking down the street, women with feathers and diamonds and furs of every possible color. As a child I'd wonder about what magical beasts had been skinned to produce a purple muff or a shockingly pink hat.

But that was not the Chamberses. They weren't old money, but they behaved like they were. I didn't know where the money came from in fact; maybe it *was* old. I just had always been told otherwise. What did I know of the politics in Atlantic City? I just kept my head down and focused on my own little world when it came to all that.

Lily stopped to speak with the rich kid so we stopped a moment after, finally joining her at her side and not being shunned completely. She had turned on the charm and I watched in my usual awe. Lily was a good kid deep down, but she was the baby of the family and had spent her whole sixteen years of life working hard to be noticed, at the expense of anyone and everyone. It was frustrating sometimes, but in moments like these when she radiated pure energy, when her smile could fuel a full city block, she was so fun to watch.

What the two of them were chatting about I hadn't any idea. I was lost in my admiration of my little sis, when suddenly all eyes were on me.

"Constance, come over here," said Lily in her lilting friendly voice. I glanced at Molly, who gave me a knowing smile, and I laughed. Oh, Lily, now we were best friends, I see.

But I did what I was told and joined them.

"Constance, right?" asked the rich kid.

"Yes." I was feeling unbelievably shy in the moment. I remembered staring at him the night before. Why had I done that? Oh, Constance.

"It's so wonderful to run into you! Are you available at the moment?" he asked.

Oh, how I hated questions like these. If I said I was, then no matter what the reason for his question, I was stuck. I couldn't say no to something with him knowing I had the time. What if his maid was sick and he needed a housekeeper for the day? Or something else of that nature, some drudgery that now I could not refuse.

I could feel my sisters staring at me.

"Yes," I replied softly.

"Excellent! Our filmmakers have already edited together footage from yesterday and I thought you'd enjoy seeing it! We are screening it for a few investors and such." He was smiling so brightly.

"Do you mean right now?" I asked.

"Yes! Since you are available after all."

After all.

We were a relatively modern family, and going somewhere with a young man by myself was not necessarily seen as a bad thing. There would also be investors evidently. But for some reason I wished very much we were the kind of family that insisted upon chaperones.

"Go, Constance! It sounds like fun! If I wasn't under the weather, I'd join you," replied Molly.

"Ah, you're the diving sister."

"Yes," said Molly with a smile. "The original."

"I'm so glad to have run into you," said the rich kid. "You're all welcome of course!"

"No," said Lily, in her direct way. "I have plans."

I looked at her, wishing I had the ability to just say no to things like she did. To just do what I wanted to do with no worries about hurting the feelings of others.

"Well, then it's just you and me," he said, turning to me. He extended his arm and I placed my hand in the crook of his elbow. I felt deeply uncomfortable but I smiled. We walked away from my sisters and I felt my face burning as we passed the spot from last night again.

"Where are we going?" I asked as calmly as I could.

"To my father's hotel, the Plaza," he replied.

"Oh," I said. That didn't make me feel any better.

"We have a projection screen set up in one of the smaller ballrooms," he added quickly. That was kind of him to clarify, and it did help a little bit.

We walked then in silence until we arrived at the hotel. Then he escorted me through the cavernous lobby, with its dark wooden front desk stretching the width of the room, rich green sofas on which patrons casually reclined, and gold accents on the walls and ceiling that glinted in the chandelier.

"This is beautiful," I said.

"You've never been inside?" he asked, sounding quite shocked.

"I've never thought to just come inside without a reason. It feels wrong."

"Well, from now on know you are always welcome!" he said. "Tell them I sent you if they say anything."

I glanced at him as he led us down a hallway with a fine brocade wallpaper.

"And . . . who should I say you are?" I asked. It was such an awkward question, and I realized I was speaking with a weird formality, like he was a prince or something. My insides burned.

The rich kid stopped in his tracks and looked at me. "I'm Bill Chambers. From the other day. I was there when you dove."

"Oh!" I said quickly. "I know who you are, I just didn't know the particulars. Like your first name."

Bill laughed then and shook his head. "I'm so sorry. How rude of me!"

"It's okay." I laughed a little too. Laughing set people at ease, and I didn't want him to feel bad.

"Am I late?" Suddenly we were joined by a young man with thin hair, panting like he'd just finished a race.

"Brant, old chum, glad you could make it!"

"I know you," I said, staring at Brant intently.

"Oh, yes, you do," he replied. He straightened his posture and even gave a little bow at the neck. "I brought you your horse yesterday."

"Of course!" I said. I didn't know why but I felt relieved to see him. Maybe it was as simple as seeing someone else who wasn't rich, or just another familiar face, but I smiled sincerely for the first time.

"Come, you two, the screening starts soon," said Bill, pulling at my arm that was still firmly attached to his.

What could we do? We obeyed.

12: BRANT

I sat next to the horse girl in the back of the room. Chairs had been set up in four rows, and there was plenty of available seating. But I didn't want to sit up front. I wasn't here for the movie. I was here for the men standing around the trolley bar, loudly laughing and clinking ice into their glasses.

"Who are they?" asked Constance, leaning over, and I felt immediately intimidated. Oh sure, I'd been around pretty girls plenty. There were a lot in my neighborhood. She actually reminded me of this girl Francine everyone had said was my sweetheart when I was eight years old. As if either of us cared about that kind of stuff. We just liked pretending we were detectives solving neighborhood mysteries.

But I had put her in the category of "celebrity" yesterday, and now we were just sitting together like this, like normal people? I definitely needed to get over this feeling if I was going to interview all types.

"They're from New York, doing business with Bill's dad."

"Are they the ones who wanted a tourist film then?" she asked.

"Is that what this is?" I asked. Of course! The pieces were all coming together now. That's why Mr. Clark had been invited to watch, that's why we'd printed that strange piece on changes in tourism post World War II this morning. Tourism, huh? What kinds of investments were needed to boost a thing like that?

"You know, this might be wrong of me to say," she said, leaning in even closer. I could feel her breath on my cheek. "But they look an awful lot like the sort of men you hear about from back in Prohibition days. The sort of people my father ended up delivering things to at very strange hours when he was a clerk around our age."

"I definitely think you're onto something," I replied. Hey, I wasn't saying it, she was.

She smiled. "Fun!"

I smiled too. Of course it wasn't really fun. It was illegal and probably pretty dangerous. We were on the fringes of something a lot darker than this cute moment sitting in a back row. Still for the two of us, us outsiders, who could help but see it as exciting or "fun"? After all I saw this as a story that could help me get my byline. She saw it as an intrigue. How did Bill see it? It was his actual life. Probably quite differently, probably as dangerous as it all actually was.

Perspective changes everything.

"Thank you all for coming!" Bill's father stood in front of

the makeshift screen with a big grin on his face, his thumbs each jammed in a jacket pocket, his fingers drumming at his torso. "This is just a first attempt, but we wanted all your feedback. After all, Atlantic City deserves the best representation because it is the best city in America."

Constance and I clapped at that but we were two of only a few who did. The guest list consisted mostly of New Yorkers. You didn't tell New Yorkers that anywhere was the best city in America if it wasn't New York.

"Let's roll the film, shall we?" said Bill's father, seeming quite unfazed. But I had a feeling he was seething inside. This was a man who liked to be liked.

The man sat down in the front row next to his son and the lights were dimmed. The projector was turned on and for a moment we were just staring at a bright square of light. Then I heard the reels spinning from behind me and the picture started.

We began on an aerial shot of the Boardwalk, of course; it was definitely the most picturesque part of the city. Had they hired a plane for it? It was very impressive to see the city from the ocean like that. The Steel Pier stuck out into the bright waves and then came butting up onto the Boardwalk. I'd always been amazed by it as a kid—how did those wooden posts going into the sea support the large building that worked its way right to the tip, getting progressively smaller as it did until it opened into fresh air? You could feel like you were alone, lost at sea, if you stood at the tip and didn't turn around. Didn't feel like there was a whole city behind you.

The camera flew over the beach with tiny people and tiny open umbrellas. Then up onto the narrow boardwalk that ran the length of the sand. The small shops that lined it all had their awnings unfurled, and the glass in their arched windows polished to a sheen. The large castle-like brick hotels rose from behind them, looking as impressive as ever. Clearly everyone had been prepared for the shoot and was showing themselves off to great effect.

Next, the film cut to a close-up of tourists walking on the Boardwalk. They walked in their summer finest, smiling and laughing and pointing at windows. Oh look, they seemed to say, James' Salt Water Taffy, cute hats, nice shoes! How delightful! It made me want to gag. It was weird watching it all without any voice-over yet. Just shots of different places and people. Nothing tying them together except for how welcoming it looked. They had done a decent job of that. They wouldn't be shooting in my neighborhood, that was for certain. They wouldn't be shooting the Northside either. Nor any of the dirty, salt-ravaged buildings on the fringes of these shots. No reality would seep into the edges of this sparkling make-believe world.

And then I was looking at that diving platform. It took me by surprise. But there was Constance standing up top, waving. And there I was, though you couldn't tell it was me, with Trix the horse. Had this just been yesterday? Watching it all on film made it feel like it had never happened at all. Or that it had been years ago.

"It's you on a horse," I said, leaning over to Constance.

"It is," she replied, sounding a little embarrassed.

"Here comes the dive." I looked at her, her profile staring straight ahead. She was lit by the screen but otherwise a dark silhouette. What did a girl like that think about?

She was suddenly looking right at me. "Do you smell smoke?"

I sniffed the air, and she was right. I turned in my seat and saw that there was smoke coming from the back of the projector. The operator and his assistant were quietly panicking, trying to fix whatever was wrong. And doing a pretty terrible job at it.

"Turn the darn thing off," I said, loudly enough that the room could hear.

Heads turned around.

"What's going on?" asked Mr. Chambers, rising in his seat. Bill was fast onto his feet as well.

"Sorry, sir, it's the projector. It's . . . just hold on, we've got this . . ." replied the operator.

Oh boy, this wasn't going to go over well.

Mr. Chambers stormed back toward us and stared down the projectionist. If looks could kill, his would do the trick. If only looks could fix projectors. He finally examined the object itself, saw the smoke, and shook his head with a scowl.

"This is a disaster," I heard him hiss. "Fix it!"

"I'm trying," said the projectionist, but with the panic in

his voice either he didn't know how or was too intimidated to think clearly. He turned to his colleague and said quietly, "Get the man from Gent in here." His colleague flew out of the room just as Bill approached.

"Can I help?" he asked.

"Sit down, Son," said his father, his tone ice-cold.

"I think I can fix it, Father," replied Bill, sounding polite and much younger in a way than I'd ever heard him sound.

I watched closely as Bill examined the projector and opened it up. I didn't know what he was doing, but I trusted he would be able to fix the thing. No sooner had he stood upright with a small smile on his face than that fella Scott came walking quickly into the room.

This would be fun, I thought, leaning back in my seat.

"I fixed it," said Bill, sounding incredibly proud of himself. It was so strange that someone so rich should care so much about such things.

Scott looked over the projector and turned it on. It whirred back to life, lighting the men standing in their seats, turning their heads into screens with dancing girls. Felt right—these men certainly seemed to always have girls on the mind.

"Good work," said Scott.

"Thank you."

"You remember what I said last night?"

"Who are you? Get out of here," said Bill's father with a wave of his hand. Scott rolled his eyes at Bill and the fellow smiled. A shared secret.

"I need to get going," said Constance then.

Bill heard that and came over. "Weren't you just magnificent?" he asked.

"It's interesting seeing myself on-screen, that's for sure," she replied with a little laugh. "You were quite impressive fixing that machine."

Bill beamed. He was coming on a bit too strong, but then again when you have that much money it doesn't matter how you come across. You generally get a positive reception.

"Thank you again," she said. "Brant, it was nice to meet you officially." I took her offered gloved hand and held it for a moment. It felt nice. She gently pulled it away and then slipped out from the row of seats and through the door.

She vanished so quickly, so effortlessly. It was a neat trick.

I thought then, maybe girls like that need to know how to disappear. Attention isn't always a good thing. I didn't understand it myself. I was tired of being invisible. I was desperate to be noticed, to be taken seriously.

But everyone's different. Look at Mr. Fix-It here. Proud as punch that he had fixed a projector. Like he'd saved the world.

We all want different things. And that's okay. Just as long as I get what I want too.

"We're ready to continue," announced Mr. Chambers.

I sure as heck was, yes.

13: CONSTANCE

I had to hurry home to get

ready for my date. It was a very strange thing for me to think and I didn't entirely hate it. I flew upstairs past my sisters helping Mother peel apples for a pie and into my room. I quickly took off my clothes and stood there in my slip, suddenly completely still, staring at the half-dozen dresses I owned. How I wished I had a proper job as a scientist or something so that I could afford to buy things that were not necessities, like pretty dresses from lovely shops.

I sat on the bed staring at my open closet. Then I turned to look at my little chemistry set. I'd barely used it, and only done the usual experiments, the easy ones they teach children, like making crystals with bicarbonate soda and mixing copper with nitric acid. How I wished that my parents hadn't insisted at sixteen we had to leave school to start earning an income. There were so many more things left to learn. But my parents had both dropped out when they had been teenagers to help support their families and they didn't see why we shouldn't.

We needed the money more than a "high-class education" as they called it. And it wasn't as if my parents hadn't stopped learning; they loved reading, and their Shakespeare and history. So why not leave school to make money and study on your own? But there was only so much you could learn without a good teacher, I found. And I had enjoyed school. A lot.

I started to resent this date now. I hardly had any free time and it didn't feel fair somehow. Yesterday had already been full doing things for other people, now today? Bill, the rich kid needing my time this morning, and a date coming up with Andrew so soon. All these boys seemed to need my time. Yesterday it was Mr. Chambers himself, though he was hardly a boy, and that was a whole other sort of thing. That wasn't a favor as much as it was an order and a rescue mission. Molly's reputation certainly would have suffered if I hadn't filled in, no matter how terrified I was at the prospect.

It was nice doing things for others; I just wished I had some time to myself once in a while. Oh, that felt selfish to think. Wasn't it? Was it? I felt almost . . . angry? But no, that was silly. I quickly buried the feeling. This was all silly. The screening had been interesting and dates are delightful. It wasn't as if I'd never been on one before, they just weren't as frequent as my sisters'. But yes, as I recalled, they were quite lovely. Fun conversation, some lovely food, butterflies in the stomach.

Then why did my butterflies feel more like dread?

I stood up in a rush, feeling a little flushed and upset,

though I couldn't understand why. I grabbed my rose dress and hastily put it on. It would do and I had nice lipstick to match.

Once made up, I fixed my hair and was feeling better until Molly knocked on my door.

"Andrew is waiting for you!" she said with a giggle.

I double-checked my appearance in the mirror and then grabbed my gray wool jacket and hat.

"You look so cute!" said Molly as I passed her in the kitchen.

"Don't be late for the show," ordered Lily, not looking up.

I rolled my eyes at Molly and Mother smacked her with the dish towel.

"Have fun, dear!"

I wanted to, I really did, but I wasn't sure I knew how. I ran downstairs and gave Mrs. Wilson a little wave and a smile as she peeked at me from behind her chain on her door. She always needed to know everything.

I stepped outside and there was Andrew waiting for me on the sidewalk with a lovely bouquet of pink roses.

"They're beautiful," I said, stunned.

"So are you," he said.

I didn't look at him, and instead purposefully examined the flowers. The compliment was silly and it sounded like something he'd said before. Not in a bad way; it just didn't feel like a compliment aimed specifically at me. But that was my ego, I supposed.

"Shall we go?" I asked.

He nodded and offered his arm. I was reminded of Bill's earlier. These boys. I took it.

We went for a nice long stroll and ended up at Reggiano's Italian Restaurant. I'd never been and I was quite excited about it as I took off my coat and he pulled out the chair for me. I sat down and took off my gloves as he sat opposite me. We were right by the window, and the glass gave off a bit of cold but it was nice to be able to watch people go by. We were otherwise alone. The restaurant had only just opened.

"It's very nice of you to accommodate my schedule," I said.

"Of course! With classes at university, schedules are all over the place. Why, I had dinner with a chum the other day at midnight because it was the only time he and I could see each other," he said with a laugh.

I laughed too. Generally, midnight was not a big deal in Atlantic City. I decided not to tell him I'd been staying out and having meals that late since I was fifteen.

"Where do you go to school?" I asked. I was instantly envious.

"I attend Rutgers. I'm planning on going into law someday," he said.

"Oh, how interesting. If I went to university I would study science," I said. I knew I shouldn't have just said that but I'd been thinking about such things and it spilled out. Why on earth would he care what I would have done if I had the chance? Such a silly hypothetical. There I went again, saying the wrong thing at the wrong time. Focus, Constance, focus.

"Science, neat," said Andrew, taking a sip of water. "I always liked science. I find law very interesting . . . I like the complexities and questions of morality."

I nodded. I was partially grateful he'd sidestepped my brazenness and continued on his own track as I should have done with the conversation. I could do this. I could be normal.

"Lawyers do seem to have such interesting lives," I said, never having met a lawyer before.

"Oh, they really do. One of my professors invited me for dinner the other day and he said the funniest thing." Andrew paused, remembering it. I smiled as he thought. The waiter arrived and hovered nearby. We all waited in anticipation.

"I can't quite remember," he said finally.

I laughed nonetheless to set him at ease. I was getting better at this. Maybe it was because this was our second encounter? Maybe it was the oddness of the morning?

"May I take your orders?" asked the waiter.

I opened the menu. "I haven't even . . ."

"We'll each have a plate of the lasagna. I'll have the merlot and the lady will have a sparkling water," said Andrew with a smile.

"Very good, sir," replied the waiter.

"Thank you," I said, handing him my menu with a smile. I wasn't against the lasagna as an idea, but I'd been rather excited to go through the menu, to imagine what everything might look and taste like. I hadn't even had a chance to op it. Oh well, that was dating.

"I'm sorry about the water," said Andrew.

"Oh, I like sparkling water," I lied.

"You must get so used to being able to drink wherever and whenever. Everything in Atlantic City is so illicit." He seemed excited by the thought.

"As a future lawyer I'm sure you don't approve," I said. I didn't mention that I really had never had any interest in drinking, and was pretty sure even when I was of age I wouldn't be too keen. Oh, maybe I'd have a sip here or there of champagne, but I liked having a clear head and I'd seen too many drunken tumbles and brawls on the Boardwalk to convince me it wasn't exactly my thing.

My statement flustered him for a moment and he carefully straightened his fork. "Oh no, I think there's a difference between the spirit and letter of the law," he said.

"Oh really? Can you explain it to me?" *Thank you, Lily, for the little lessons you've taught me along the way*, I thought. Asking a date to explain something definitely raised their spirits and filled the time. Andrew was no exception.

The rest of the dinner continued without incident. I enjoyed my lasagna even if it wouldn't have been my first choice, and was able to eat it quite peacefully since he took up most of the conversation. He was interesting at moments, and I did find the question of right and wrong and the law kind of compelling. I wished I could have told him a bit about my chemistry set but I didn't want to interrupt him. He was having a grand time talking to me.

We finished and he paid for us. He helped me with my coat. Then we walked over to the Oceanview and parted ways in front of the hotel. As we stood there looking at each other, I felt those butterflies from last night. But I also wasn't sure I wanted to kiss him. I could tell he wasn't sure if he should kiss me.

"Did you know I do horse diving on occasion?" I asked him.

He stared and blinked once and then said, "What?"

"Thank you for dinner. It was wonderful." I extended my hand and he took it, still confused but warmly so. I smiled but it was more to myself than anything. If he had only asked a single question about me.

As I headed up the stairs, he called out after me, "May I see you again?"

A couple chorus girls near me giggled.

"Yes," I replied. Why not another chance? He was decent enough.

And I stepped inside the hotel.

14: BRANT

After the screening I was feeling

inspired. I was fast at work at the spare typewriter at the office. I could tell Mr. Clark was watching me. Not all the time. But he'd pop his head out of his office and squint at me. He didn't want me writing this story. Not when Mr. Chambers was an investor in the paper itself. But this was too good. Those men from New York. I didn't recognize any of them yet, but there was a good chance if I did some cross-referencing in the files . . . if they weren't mob affiliated I'd eat my own hat. And I only had one hat, so that meant something!

I left that afternoon practically skipping down the street like my little sister. I had an idea then, just to head back toward the club. Maybe I'd run into Bill again, or his father, or those men. Then I realized, no, the Atlantic Plaza hotel. It was by far the grandest hotel Mr. Chambers owned and there was no way he wasn't putting up his guests in one of their prime ocean-view suites. I'd stake out the lobby.

I turned on my heel and made my way toward the

waterfront. As always, the air got colder and windier as I got closer to the water. Some days it made you feel frigid, but today it felt invigorating. I was ready to take on the world!

I arrived at the Plaza and awkwardly smiled at the doorman as I passed through into the large marble foyer. Sure, it had been fine when Bill had been with me this morning, but on my own I suddenly felt very out of place. I had to admit I didn't tend to visit these buildings much, even though I supposed it was free to do so. They intimidated me, sure. But also the ostentatious wealth, the expense of having marble imported, and a giant cavernous space filled with nothing, while others lived paycheck to paycheck and were barely able to put food on their tables, made me uncomfortably twitchy.

"Can I help you, sir?" asked a man in a tailored jacket with "AP" embroidered on the lapel.

Right. This was the other reason. When you looked and dressed like me, you weren't going to be allowed to loiter for too long.

"Just waiting to pick up a package," I replied. "I'll just stay back here."

"Shall I call up to the room, sir?" asked the man, clearly not believing me.

"No, they said not to disturb them."

The man looked at me with one eyebrow raised.

"I can wait outside," I said, and backed away slowly. I passed once more through the door held open by the doorman and he gave me a sympathetic shrug.

I crossed the street and stared out into the ocean. The sky was blue and bright, the sun was just beginning its descent and gave everything a warm glow. The water looked almost welcoming. You could be deceived it was as warm as the tropics if not for the cold wind blowing.

I turned and leaned against the railing of the Boardwalk, watching the entrance to the hotel. It was cold, but it was just as good. Besides, my excitement was helping keep me warm inside.

"Brant?"

Someone was calling up to me from the beach below. I looked down over the railing and saw Bill waving up at me. That was an unexpected and very welcome sight.

"Bill!" I called out, waving back. "What are you doing there, pal?"

"Collecting shells. Come down and join me," he said.

Collecting shells? That didn't seem like the hobby of a rich kid, but then again what did I know about the hobbies of rich kids.

"Sure!"

I made my way to the stairs and joined him on the beach. The sand slipped under my shoes, and I struggled to make my way over to him.

"Shells?" I asked once I finally made it.

Bill nodded and held up his hand. He had half a dozen or so shells, mostly small, but quite detailed and unbroken. Finding good unbroken shells did take some work.

"Funny seeing you here," he said.

"I needed some air before heading home."

He nodded. I wondered now if he trusted me. I thought we'd had a good thing going, but it hadn't occurred to me that he might not be entirely falling for my friend act.

I turned and pointed over toward a smaller hotel a few buildings down from the Plaza. "That's your dad's also, right?"

He nodded again. "That one, and that one, and that one." He pointed them out as they disappeared into the distance along the Boardwalk.

"What's that like?"

"What's what like?"

"Having a dad who owns a city?" I pulled my coat tight around me and started walking a little in place.

"Honestly?" he asked.

"Why would you not be completely honest with a stranger you just met yesterday?" I asked back with a grin.

He finally smiled.

"I try not to think about it. I want to just live my own life. I don't want to own all this. It's too much work and too much . . ." He paused. I waited for him. Didn't push. "Sometimes it's dangerous."

"Dangerous?"

He gave me a look. "You know what I mean."

Did I? Was he confirming what I was thinking about those men last night? "Those men from New York," I said.

But he didn't say anything. Just looked back toward the sea.

"I get wanting to do your own thing. Have your own dreams. Why do older folks try to push things on us? They make up their minds about everything now that they're old but when they were young, they were rebels." I said this thinking about my aunt and uncle. Thinking about how they took me in. Thinking about what they sacrificed for that. I felt a little guilty.

"Exactly," said Bill. "Exactly."

"I feel a little bad," I said.

"You do? Why?" asked Bill.

"All this talking about dreams and such, and I told you not to pursue yours." Show some empathy, remember the details, and make them feel special.

Bill smiled. "Oh, that. That's just silliness. What purpose could it serve. Besides, you were right, I don't want to take employment from anyone else."

"Or maybe they have no plans to hire anyone, but you were the exception. You know," I said, an idea just occurring to me, "you could offer to work for free. A small business always can use the help. It would be more like, I dunno, a charity act."

"Charitable act," he said. He seemed to think about it for a moment but then dismissed it. "Well, it's neither here nor there. I should be heading inside. There's a dinner I'm obliged to go to."

"With those same men?" I asked. Bill nodded, looking a little distracted. "If you'd like company . . ." He looked at me, confused. "I'm just saying that I have no plans."

"Brant," Bill said, frowning slightly, "desperation isn't a good look."

"Oh, I didn't mean to push." Too far, Brant, too far.

"I know. I'm sorry. I'm just tired of people wanting things from me. I know you aren't like that."

"I understand," I said. I felt like I'd just tried to capture a stray dog by grabbing it by its scruff. Next time, I told myself, next time. "Well, have a nice dinner!"

"Thank you," said Bill. He looked at his hand for a moment, then turned and threw the shells out into the water. He rubbed his hands together, gave me one last nod, and made his way along the beach back to the stairs.

I sat down in the cold sand and pulled my jacket collar up.

This always happened. I always went just a little too far. Folks gave me an inch, and I took a mile, as the saying went. My uncle said it was a good quality, especially as a reporter, but I guess sometimes it's not. Especially with skittish marks like Bill.

Next time I'd do better. Next time I'd get the scoop.

15: BILL

I was standing in a dark little street made darker by the setting sun hidden behind the dingy gray buildings. I looked around. Time had slipped away from me again. I couldn't remember the exact moment I'd decided to bail on dinner, decided to follow an address on a business card. But here I was. And so I must have. I double-checked the card in my hand and then looked up at the address in front of me. This was where the Gent headquarters was supposed to be, but I was looking at an empty storefront with dusty windows. I looked around. I was starting to feel worried, a little fearful. Was this really the place? Maybe I should just head back to the hotel, actually join my father and those men for dinner like I'd told Brant I was doing. But no. No, I just couldn't stomach that. I knocked tentatively. After waiting a few moments I knocked harder. And then finally I grabbed the doorknob just as the door itself was flung open. My arm practically dislocated itself from my shoulder and I stumbled forward, falling onto the ground.

"Lookie lookie, it's the film projector kid. Mr. Fuse Box." Scott was looking down at my prostrate body with a smirk on his face.

"Bad timing," I said, standing and brushing the dirt off my front.

"I'd say it's perfect timing myself. That was a pratfall worthy of Buster Keaton."

"Well then, good, I aim to make a positive first impression," I replied. I stepped back into the street, letting Scott out of the building and watching as he locked up shop.

"Hate to break it to you, kid, but this is your third impression," he said.

"Right, right." I was not usually at a loss for words, especially not in a business context, but right then I felt very . . . well . . . silly. And very awkward.

"So, what can I do you for?" he asked.

"I would like to take you up on your offer. I'd like to learn. And I would do it for free. I don't need the money." That felt stupid to say the moment I'd said it. It felt like bragging. I hadn't meant it to. I wanted to sound charitable, like Brant had suggested. Instead I just sounded smug.

"Well, I'll tell you, the boss will be thrilled. You've got skills, kid, and also, free is, well, free is pretty fantastic. Can't do better than that."

"Unless I paid you," I joked. Scott looked for a moment suddenly like the idea had merit. Shoot. Why did I say that? "Just don't tell my father. He believes that hard work should be rewarded properly and fairly, and he doesn't always understand that that can mean more than just money."

Scott nodded. "Of course. Not sure when I'd be having this intimate chat with your dad, but I'll make sure to not tell him that."

"Thank you." Still feeling awkward. "So, do I get the job?"

"Let's see, we've agreed you'll work for nothing, and you're talented and motivated. I guess, sure, we could give it a shot." He grinned. "How about you come with me and meet the boss?"

"Great, perfect, I'd love that."

❤❤❤❤❤❤❤❤❤❤❤❤❤❤❤❤❤❤❤❤

I soon changed my mind as we sped through the city streets in the man's truck, the side painted with large letters: "GENT." It was as if he thought he was on some racetrack, taking corners at speeds that made my stomach turn, and I felt fairly certain his old clunker would fall apart on the next pothole. Or at least I'd lose some of my teeth from knocking together when we did.

"Where are we going?" I thought I knew Atlantic City well, but this insane driving had completely thrown me.

"Fantastic jazz bar. It's called the Jive Dive," replied Scott, wrenching the wheel and spinning us almost 180 degrees in order to take a very normal right turn. I felt queasy.

"I've never heard of that one," I said.

"It's on the Northside," he replied.

"Oh." I didn't say anything else. I worried if I did I might throw up.

"You okay with that?" he asked, looking at me.

Please stop looking at me, look at the road. A young woman with her child was crossing the street in front of us. Oh, this was right out of a film. "Of course," I said.

"Because if it makes you uncomfortable . . ."

"Why would it make me uncomfortable . . . oh dear god!"

Scott looked back at the road and casually swerved around the woman and gave her a friendly wave.

"Well, okay then! You'll love the boss. Just so you know, he can be a bit prickly. Been dealing with a lot of stuff in New York," he said.

"New York?" I asked.

"Got fired, got the job back, didn't want it back, it's a whole thing. He might tell you about it or not. Just let him talk or let him be. Just let him . . ."

"Let him take the lead, I understand. Most bosses are like that."

The rest of the ride was mercifully quiet as Scott raced the streets to the Northside. I held fast to the underside of my seat and tried to just breathe my way through the experience. When we finally stopped and I was able to peel my way out of the truck, I almost knelt on the pavement to kiss the ground.

"This way!" said Scott, completely unaware of the ordeal he had put me through, or the opposite. I couldn't tell.

I joined him as we walked along the busy streets to a small

club with a bright marquee out in front. We made our way inside. The club was small and dark, but the effect was cozy and intimate, not dingy. The footlights uplit a small stage at the far end where a jazz trio was playing, and each table had a candle flickering away on it. The place was very casual, quite the opposite of my father's club. It also allowed both men and women, which was, I thought, much nicer.

I followed Scott to a table in a back corner, a curved dark-red upholstered banquet on one side. Sitting there was a large formidable-looking man, a scowl on his face. Oh, how I hoped this was some bodyguard and not the boss himself.

"Hey there, boss!" said Scott, sliding in beside the large man. Wonderful. "This is the kid I was telling you about."

I quickly took off my hat and held out my hand. "Hi! I'm Bill Chambers."

The man looked at me for a moment, looked at Scott, and then looked back at me. Then slowly and with obvious reluctance he reached out and shook my hand. "Thomas Connor," he said.

"Well, Mr. Connor, I'm really excited about this opportunity. It seems to me that Gent is doing some truly innovative things."

Mr. Connor stared at me and then once again looked at Scott. "What did you tell him?"

Scott raised his hands and laughed. "Hey now, nothing! Just that we were happy to hire someone to work for us for free."

"For free?"

"Yes."

Mr. Connor looked at me again and I suddenly felt the urge to run away. To just leave the club and hop in Scott's truck and drive it all the way home.

"Why would you want to work for free?"

"I'm rich," I said. I said it just like that. In the way I might have when I was around seven years old and learned the difference between me and most people.

Mr. Connor stared at me. Then he shook his head. "Sit down already."

I sat quickly on the other side of him on the banquet. It felt oddly intimate, all three of us sitting curved like this, next to one another. I tried to sit as close to the edge as possible.

A waitress arrived then. "Can I get you fellas something to drink?"

"I'll have a whiskey sour," said Scott.

The waitress looked at me. "Just a soda, thanks."

She left and there was a long pause. I would say it was silent except it wasn't. The band was playing something bright and cheerful, the customers at the other tables were loud and raucous. It was a very lively scene. Except in this dark corner. In this dark corner, things were, well, uncomfortable.

"Did everything go well last night?" Scott asked Mr. Connor then.

Mr. Connor nodded. "As well as could be expected."

"I can't believe you did that. After everything that man did to you."

"Not now, Scott."

The waitress returned with our drinks and I was grateful to have something to occupy myself during this, the world's most awkward job interview.

"Just find it strange," said Scott, sipping his drink.

"A man has responsibilities. Even after everything. It was a good thing. It was the right thing to do. To get it out of there."

"I think you should have sunk that ship. Just sent it all to the bottom of the ocean."

"And you know what would have happened then, do you? You know how the ink and seawater would have..." He stopped. I was remembered. Mr. Connor turned to me. "You like to fix things?"

It was so sudden, I just nodded.

"Well, kid, you better be as good as Scott says you are. There are a lot of things that need fixing out there."

"Is that a metaphor?" I asked.

"No."

"Right."

Except I was pretty certain it was. What on earth were they discussing? It captured my imagination, that was for sure. It struck a chord in my gut, and I felt, well, a little frightened. But very intrigued.

"So I, uh, got the job?" I asked.

Mr. Connor nodded. "Why not." Then he laughed to himself. "Sure. Why not."

THE MACHINE

Anxious anticipation.
Of something unknown.
We're here waiting. We can't see anything in the dark.
But we can feel it.
We aren't alone.

16: BILL

Time passes. Always moving forward no matter what else is happening. Sometimes you feel like you're running to catch up, other times you feel like it is pushing you forward so fast you will trip over your own feet. It passes, and moments that have significance stand out, but the rest, the rest is a series of quick pictures. Snapshots of a life lived. My time jumps. Ignore the concern, ignore the bits that tie things together.

I really wish now that I had paid more attention. I wish that the weeks that passed working for Gent had been something I'd been more considerate to imprint on my mind. But it all blurs together now. The days were so similar, even if the jobs were not. I'd wake up, have breakfast, and read from a new book. I'd go to the dusty unnamed storefront and meet with Scott and we'd be out all day to fix things. It might be as simple as a fuse box, or as fascinating as some theater lights. We might have to climb the ladder up to the top of a marquee or climb down into a cellar to work on a generator. It was all a lark.

I saw Brant a few times too. That lad had a way of suddenly appearing. Had I been my father I would have thought he was stalking me. He was pretty swell, and liked good conversation. So I didn't mind his company, as unprepared as I was each time he magically appeared.

17: CONSTANCE

The thing they tell you is that

love conquers all. I always thought that meant that no matter what happened in a relationship, if you were truly in love, it didn't matter. But what I was discovering was how being in a relationship meant that nothing else mattered. Not to me, but to everyone else. If I was late to help the girls get ready, they giggled and blamed Andrew. Lily suddenly was interested in conversation, talking about her many suitors and asking if Andrew would have done such and such terrible thing, and fawning over flowers he sent me.

Even my parents, who had always been so supportive of me and my quiet ways, seemed so pleased. If Andrew was taking me out on the town for the evening, suddenly I no longer needed to clean up after dinner.

Worst of all, my new chemistry set sat there collecting dust, being pushed to the side as little boxes with necklaces and broaches filled my desk. Love was literally conquering my hobbies, my interests, my passions.

Love conquered all. All things. All that mattered was love.

There was, of course, only one problem. *I* wasn't in love with *him*. *He* was in love with *me*. It was *his* love pushing everything else to the side. It was *his* love that mattered most. To my family. To everyone who smiled knowingly at me.

Everyone was so pleased. So who was I to ruin their joy? And Andrew was perfectly acceptable. Interesting in his own way, kind, respectful. I supposed I would have to marry him. That seemed the way of things.

What could I say? How could I express the resentment I felt in this situation? How could I hurt all these people? I wished then that I was rich like Bill, and none of this would matter then.

But it probably would.

A girl needs a suitor. A girl needs to marry. That is her job.

I picked up one of the small glass vials of liquid from my dusty chemistry set. I raised my arm to throw it against the wall. I imagined how satisfying the shattering would sound. How pleasing the liquid exploding everywhere would look. Then I sighed and placed it gently back in the box.

I made a point of learning Bill's

routine. It was easy. The guy was a full-time Gent employee now. Thanks to me. Only problem was that meant he was spending a lot less time with his fancy father and his formidable friends. What was the story now? Rich kid volunteers to fix the city his father broke? Not a bad headline, but not front-page material.

There was not much I could do now. I just had to keep up with the friendship. I knew someday, somewhere the story would appear. This kid had too much surrounding him to not slip and fall headfirst into something. Meanwhile I had to thank Mr. Clark for taking me under his wing. I was editing the obituaries now, officially out of the mail room. It wasn't much, but it meant a jump in pay, and you know, it was kind of interesting reading about the lives people lead before they die. Most deaths aren't front-page news; it just happens as naturally as being born. People are in our lives and then gone. Kind of like my parents, I guess, not that I'd ever known them long enough to notice that they were gone.

So yeah, it's neat to see the lives lived. The kids, grand-kids, even great-grandkids sometimes. It also can get pretty repetitive. Which again, maybe that's a neat thing too. Maybe it shows that most people are living simple, predictable lives and are pretty happy.

I wondered about that. Was it because I had such an unusual upbringing that I didn't think much about a wife and a family in my future? That all I cared about was making it above the fold? Or was it that the future didn't seem to exist for me? It was all just this black void out there, just an inky-black void.

Well, that was a creepy thought.

I shook my head and went back to editing.

19: BILL

It was 5:00 p.m. and already

dark outside. I was standing out in front of the empty Gent storefront, shivering a little in my long black wool winter coat. I was trying to lock up but my fingers were numb with the cold. I should have worn gloves.

"You all alone?" asked an ominous voice behind me.

I spun on my heel, my heart beating fast. A large figure towered over me, and when I recognized him, it didn't do much to assuage my fear.

"Hi there, Mr. Connor," I said, feeling intimidated as I always did around him. I hadn't seen him in just over two weeks, since that evening at the club. He'd gone back to New York and that had been that. Or so I'd thought.

"Bill." We stared at each other. Then: "Where's Scott?"

"He went home early. His baby is sick." It felt like a lie, except it was the truth. There was just something about how Mr. Connor stared at me that made me feel like everything I was saying was somehow inappropriate.

"Great," he said with a hefty sigh.

"What's wrong?" I asked, then immediately doubted if anything was wrong in the first place and that I shouldn't make such assumptions about people, especially large individuals who looked like they could tear me in half.

"I need help. But it's . . ." He stopped. He stared at me hard. I raised my eyebrows and tried to smile a little to show him I was a reliable sort of person who was of no threat to him whatsoever.

"Can I be of service?" I asked.

He continued to stare at me.

"I've been really improving, I think you'd be impressed." Why was I insisting so hard? There was something about Mr. Connor that made me want to impress him.

"It's not about talent. I'm sure you've got skills, kid. It's about trust."

"Trust?"

"Can you be trusted?"

I was mildly offended. "Of course."

"With secrets, knowing you can't tell a single soul, and if you do I'll make you regret it."

Well, with a threat like that, who was I to say no? "I'm very good at keeping secrets." I wasn't about to go into how I kept secret all the things I knew my father got up to and how he'd earned all his fortune. Because, well, it was a secret after all.

Mr. Connor nodded. He seemed to understand. It wasn't like rumors about my father didn't swirl around Atlantic City like the waves in the ocean.

"Then come with me," he said.

We drove to a part of the city filled with garages and packaging factories. A place of low-roofed buildings and dirt and soot. It was all purpose-built, no attention to details that might please the eye. We pulled up to a brick building with a nondescript door and got out. I looked around. We were at the edge of town. Not quite on the water but I could hear waves in the distance. The smell of oil and gasoline mingled in the air. This was a place for hard work. Our path was overrun with dead weeds; ours was the only car parked in the empty lot.

We entered the building. Mr. Connor flicked on the lights and only half came to life. We were in one large, empty room with a few hooks hanging from the ceiling.

"Meatpacking?" I asked, looking around.

"Once upon a time, yes. About twenty years ago."

Twenty years ago. Ah. I understood now. "There's more to this building than it seems, isn't there?"

Mr. Connor shook his head but somehow was agreeing with me and led me to a set of stairs toward the back. We descended to a small landing with shelves along the opposite wall. He quickly opened the top of the newel post and pushed something. The wall to our side suddenly started to open. It was heavy and the gears were grinding hard. If I was right, and I was sure I was, this was a twenty-year-old door used during Prohibition. The likely thing behind it? Alcohol production. I didn't ask though. I figured I'd learn the truth soon enough.

We walked into a small, dank room and then through

an opening in the wall and down another creaky flight of stairs. It opened up into a large room. This one had so much more equipment in it, almost as if it was left behind in haste. There were large tables, and sinks along the wall, baskets hanging from the ceiling. There was a huge old icebox with a chain around its middle, and bottles scattered about on the floor. All this I noticed and processed but I hardly looked at. I hardly looked around at all. I just stared.

At the machine.

I'd never seen a machine like this in my life. It was huge. With pipes running in and out of it but not connected to anything else. It looked new but used. The metal had a sheen to it, but the seams were rusting a little. And there was this black substance speckled everywhere. Oil perhaps?

"What is that?"

"The Ink Machine," replied Mr. Connor, approaching it.

"What does it do?" I asked, following him.

"No time for questions. I need help welding this side together." He had already taken off his coat and was rolling up his sleeves.

I nodded and followed suit. "What do I do?"

"You need to pull out the panel on the other side and pull down the lever to control the internal pressure." He passed me a screwdriver while settling down beside the machine.

I walked around to the other side of the giant machine and found the panel. I quickly unscrewed it and reached inside. "Do I pull it now?"

"Yup," replied Mr. Connor from the other side. I pulled on the lever and there was a sudden explosion of light. I thought I had caused it until I remembered that Mr. Connor was welding on the other side. Sparks flew; I could see them rise over the top of the machine. I looked back down at my hand inside the machine and leaned down to peek inside. It was dark as you'd imagine. I could hear the welding on the other side. Then silence.

"What is an Ink Machine?" I tried again, now that we were working. Maybe some casual conversation would inspire him to answer me.

"Something that no one should have ever invented," he replied.

"Oh." That didn't make me feel good. "Why not?"

There was another burst of sound and flash of light. I waited there, holding on to that lever, for it to be over, for an answer. My excitement had been poisoned and now turned sour.

"You ask too many questions," replied Mr. Connor. "You can release the lever and close up the panel."

I looked back into the machine as I slowly released the lever. I heard a small popping hiss and then I was sprayed in the face. I stood up sputtering. As I backed away from the machine, Mr. Connor was suddenly beside me, handing me a rag.

"Wipe that stuff off quick," he said.

I nodded and did so, cleaning my face carefully. I looked at the rag, black with the same oil or whatever that was speckled on the machine. The rag was snatched quickly out of my hand, as Mr. Connor stuffed it into his pocket. He said nothing, just turned and stared at the giant metal beast before us.

So I did too. Gazing at it. Trying to figure it out, to deconstruct it, to understand it.

"The man who built this machine thought he was revolutionizing an industry. Instead it created a monster," said Mr. Connor then.

"What do you mean?" I asked, turning to him.

"You don't know what a monster is?" replied Mr. Connor, not looking at me, still staring at the machine in front of us.

"I know monsters. The Jabberwock." My father. That was the answer I wanted to say.

"The what?"

"I'm rereading *Alice's Adventures in Wonderland*."

"Oh, the children's book." He said it dismissively. "Do you know what happens when a man makes a machine and a machine makes a monster?"

I shook my head now. I was speechless. This man who barely put two words together in conversation now spoke in strange twisted metaphors. It was unnerving.

"The man loses everything."

"I see."

Mr. Connor sighed hard. "You don't. You don't see. No one does. He stole it from him. Then begged him to come back. Begged him to bring it here. I should destroy it."

"Who are you talking about?"

"A man. A very dangerous man. But here I am. It's my fault, so it's my responsibility."

"Mr. Connor, I'm sorry if this is rude," I said, "but I am very confused. Who are you talking about?"

Mr. Connor laughed. "Straight speaking. I don't hate that about you, kid. I'm talking about a Mister Drew."

"Oh." Why did that name sound familiar to me?

"And me."

"And you?" It made sense then. "You invented this."

"I did. It's my fault."

"When you say monster . . ."

Mr. Connor shook his head and then suddenly he was done with the conversation. He turned and made his way back toward the stairs, turning off the lights as he did so.

I stood for a moment in the dark, watching his retreating back. A shiver ran up my spine. I turned to look at the machine once more. And then quickly followed him.

20: CONSTANCE

"Miss Gray, this is exactly what I was looking for," Mac the stage manager said. We were looking at beautiful clouds of fog filling the stage, making everything appear quite magical, even the mop and bucket standing front and center. "You are a humdinger of a gal sometimes."

"Thanks, Mac!" I said. I couldn't believe it! Finally after all the days with Andrew, I had been given a whole weekend to myself. He had been so apologetic that he had to visit his family. I had reassured him that distance makes the heart grow fonder, but inside mine was bursting with joy. Time to just do whatever I wanted. Time to finally play with my chemistry set. To create fake weather systems.

Or at least a fabulous stage fog that looked fantastic in the lights.

"You keep making this, I'll pay you for the materials, and a little extra for that noggin of yours," said Mac, hands in pockets, nodding happily.

"Best of all, it won't stink up the costumes," I added.

"Okay, okay, you'd better skedaddle out of here. The girls are going to need you!"

I nodded and jumped up onto the stage as light as a feather. I ran backstage and stood in the wings for a moment. Then I did a little jive and clapped my hands together. I was so happy. I didn't know I could feel quite this happy. Nothing else had done it before this. Not horse diving, or boys, or helping out with the costumes. Making something like this, that was magical.

No, it was science.

I barely heard a word anyone said to me backstage. Though I did notice Chloe say something about me being in love and lost in the clouds. I found that almost insulting, but I didn't say anything. I never said anything. Besides, for some reason it didn't upset me. Because at least I knew it wasn't true. And maybe I was lost in the clouds, lost in the clouds of man-made fog! Or, actually, girl-made fog!

I stayed in the dressing room during the show, cleaning up and just overall feeling proud of myself, and then happily entered the whirlwind of activity after the performance, undoing buttons and collecting items that needed to be cleaned. I was in such an incredible mood I wondered if it would ever go away. I even said yes when Chloe pressured me again to go out, and borrowed another sparkly dress.

"Would you like to try my lipstick?" she asked. Normally when asked I'd say no. Not that I was often asked my opinion on my makeovers. But this time, for some reason, I said yes.

"I would, thank you."

I carefully put it on. It was bright and bold, and made me a little nervous, but I was feeling bright and bold so I took in a deep breath and admired the look instead.

"Constance, there's a boy waiting for you," said Nancy, poking her head in from the hall to the stage door.

And then there it was. My good feeling popped like a balloon. My face fell. I had thought Andrew was visiting his parents in Bridgehampton this weekend. I nodded.

"Are you okay?" asked Chloe, noticing my expression.

"Why do boys ruin everything?" I asked, standing up and straightening my dress.

"The right boys don't," she replied. She gave me a little squeeze from behind. "It's okay to decide you don't like a boy. It's all about finding the right one."

I nodded. I wasn't sure there would be a right one. Right now I had a crush on my chemistry set. It wasn't that I didn't like boys, and didn't get all aflutter around them. I just felt that right now that wasn't my priority. Even if for everyone else it seemed to be.

I grabbed my things and made my way to the stage door. I took in a deep breath and smiled and then opened it.

"Bill?" I asked, surprised.

"I'm so happy you're here! But why weren't you onstage?" he asked, all smiles.

"I'm not a performer," I replied, still stunned as I stepped out into the restaurant.

"But the horse!"

"Oh, that was a favor for Molly," I replied. "I prefer to help out behind the scenes."

Bill nodded as if that sounded perfectly reasonable. "Can I buy you a drink? It's so wonderful to see you!"

I noticed some of the girls lingering by the edge of the stage, watching. I wondered what it must be like to be a Chambers. To always have people observing you. But it was strangely nice to see him.

"Yes, please," I replied.

He led me past the tables by the foot of the stage and up onto the higher platform toward the back where generally rich benefactors watched the show but didn't really. They just chatted with one another while being served by our most attentive waiters. A performance of some kind went on in the distance.

This of course is where Mr. Chambers would sit with his friends. This is where Bill directed me and pulled out a chair for me at an empty table.

"Were you here alone?" I asked, sitting.

"Yes," he replied. "I like to do things alone. It's weird, I know," he added, shaking his head.

"Not that weird," I replied with a smile. I understood. I wished I had that privilege. It would be nice, just to have the time to not be around anyone.

"So, what do you do backstage then?" he asked, flagging down a waiter, who arrived almost instantaneously. I supposed he had been waiting and watching for Bill Chambers to raise his hand.

"Oh, it's not exciting. I help with costumes. Changing into them, quick changes, cleaning them sometimes."

"Sorry to interrupt you. What would you like to drink?" asked Bill.

"Oh, uh, just a soda," I said, turning to the waiter.

"Two sodas!" he said to the waiter. Then he turned back to me. "You were saying?"

"Was I?" I replied. "Oh yes, it was just about costumes."

"Well, it sounds fascinating. The world of backstage has always been so intriguing to me," said Bill.

I laughed because it was quite the opposite. Messy, and smelly. Did I dare tell him that girls smelled? "But oh!" I said suddenly.

"Yes?"

"I did something amazing today," I added. Why not share after all? That bubbly excited feeling was flooding me again. "I came up with the perfect recipe for fog!"

"For fog?" He looked confused.

"For fog, for the stage, that is. I made it at home, I have this little chemistry set, it's nothing fancy, but I made it. And I did it. And Mac is going to use it." I grinned wide.

"That's wonderful!" said Bill just as the sodas arrived. "Perfect timing!" He held up his glass and I did too, following his lead. "Here's to inventing things!"

I couldn't stop smiling, "To inventing things!" We sipped our drinks. "I know you like machines and how they work. I saw you the other day with that projector," I said.

stion about him.

I nodded even though I couldn't think of the last time anyone had wanted to ask me about anything.

So I told him. I told him how it all started in school when I was around seven playing with the classic volcano experiment. From that point on I thought it was fascinating that you could mix things to create other things.

We got another soda and also some appetizers and then I found myself talking about my family and how I loved them but I couldn't be them, and how horse diving terrified me ("But you were so good at it!") and how I liked being alone like he did.

Eventually it got to a point where I genuinely wanted to know more about him, and I wondered if he was trying only to talk about me to avoid that subject. He couldn't truly be interested.

"Well, it's just because I'm not that interesting," he said. "My life is all planned out for me. I will take over my father's businesses eventually. Sometimes I go into the office with him and he forces me to attend these awful parties with these awful people. I need to get to know who's important. But honestly, I'm like you."

"Not possible," I said.

"Very possible. I like science too, as you know. How to fix things. If only I could just work for Gent forever." He leaned forward. "Can I tell you a secret?"

"Absolutely!"

"I've been volunteering with them. I'm a handyman!" he said with a laugh.

"No!"

"Yes! I go out every day with this man named Scott, and we fix things. And I just love it. I believe they think I'm quite good, too. The other day his, I guess 'our,' boss, Mr. Connor, took me to help him on a top secret project."

"Ooh," I said. I was giddy. His excitement added up onto my own, and it was such a nice feeling.

"It's the most incredible machine I've ever seen and I have no idea what it does," said Bill, wide-eyed. "It's both terrifying and beautiful at the same time."

"That sounds so interesting!" I replied, my eyes also quite wide. There was something a little different about Bill tonight. He was always enthusiastic and kind to me, but this was something else. I couldn't figure it out. It was almost manic. I noticed a small black speck of dirt or something just below his left eye. I found myself fixating on it until Bill slammed his soda glass on the table, spilling the stuff over his hand. I nearly jumped out of my skin!

"You like science!" he said. "I'll show you!"

"I do like science," I replied. "Okay!" Why not? This was too much fun and quite exciting.

We stood up, and Bill flagged down the waiter as I attempted to put on my coat. For some reason one of the sleeves refused to behave.

"I'll help, I'll help!" said Bill. Yes, he was quite giddy. It gave me pause, but only for a moment. It was hard to suppress the joy at being taken seriously for once by someone outside my family.

Together we managed to get me in my coat and then he grabbed my hand and pulled me across the room. I was laughing so hard and I didn't care that people were staring.

Today was such a good day.

21: BRANT

I watched Bill and Constance

from the shadows in the room. I felt like a spy. The two of them were having a grand old time, especially Bill. He was behaving in a weird way. I would have thought maybe he was drunk if they hadn't been drinking sodas the whole time. It was strange. Something was up. And I was going to figure out what.

They stood up and I quickly tried to flag down a waiter. I was ignored. Of course. So, I dropped five bucks on the table and quickly got up to follow them. I didn't know where they were going or why, but I needed a story. I needed a way in. I had overheard Bill saying something about a machine, and that was all I needed to know. Those men from New York, now a new kind of machine? It all had to be connected.

That's how it was then. Making connections without any proof. But not noticing the things right in front of my face. Not until it was too late.

I followed them at a distance, leaving the theater and then walking through the foyer of the hotel. This one was far less grand than the Plaza and I felt more comfortable here. There were also a lot of columns holding up the roof, or at least pretending to, so I could hide behind them. Kind of like a creep. And watch. Also like a creep.

They left the hotel and flagged down a cab. Shoot. I quickly made my way to the exit and outside just as they got in. I flagged one down myself and wondered if I could go back inside and grab those five bucks. But I had a bit more cash on me. It was all the cash I had on me for the rest of the week. This had better be worth it.

I got into the cab and said, "Follow that car!" I couldn't help but smile. That was not something you got to say a lot. It was fun. The cabbie for his part didn't seem as thrilled at the idea of chasing someone.

"Really?" he asked, turning in his seat to look at me.

"No joke, friend," I replied. "I really need to follow them."

The cabbie sighed and turned back. He pulled out and started tailing them. I wondered if he got asked this a lot. I thought it was just something from the movies, but here I was chasing a car, so circumstances must arise for other folks as well. Funny to think about.

We chased the car through the city to the edge of town. When they pulled over, we drove past them and around the corner. The cabbie knew to do that without me even having to ask. I probably wouldn't have thought to do that in the first place. Clever man. I paid him and tipped him and he gave me a nod. "Good luck, mate," he said.

I smiled.

I retraced my steps and Bill and Constance were gone. I quickly jogged over to the building they'd been dropped off at. There was a single door in a wide wall.

Sure, why not?

I opened it slowly and carefully and looked around. It was a large empty room with some hooks hanging from the ceiling. Bill and Constance were nowhere to be seen.

Then I heard a laugh.

It came from somewhere toward the back of the room.

I raced across the open space to the staircase and looked down.

I could hear them talking.

Okay.

I'd wait, just for a moment.

This was thrilling. This was what I'd been waiting for.

Finally.

22: CONSTANCE

A stairway to nowhere. I'd been
to my fair share of former speakeasies. They were the kind
of places that delighted showgirls and drew the fascination of
rich potential suitors. So I assumed there had to be more to
this empty cement room.

I walked up to one wall and looked at it closely, running
my fingers across it, trying to find a hidden door.

"Do you want me to just show you?" asked Bill. His energy
was still off, calmer now but strange, almost antsy.

I shook my head. I didn't want to admit that these kinds
of puzzles frustrated me, but I wanted to figure it out nonetheless. The cold air from outside had helped clear some of my
excitement and I was feeling mildly more focused now. I could
do this.

I took a step back when I realized that there were no secret
doors cut into the walls somehow. Which could only mean one
thing, "The wall *is* the door."

Bill smiled a knowing smile and I sighed inwardly but

smiled back. Men enjoyed smiling knowing smiles around girls. Most of the time it was because one of the chorus girls would pretend not to know what a particular drink was, or food dish, so that these young men could share their wisdom. But this time at least it meant something. It was a smile indicating that Bill knew something that I did not.

"So then . . ." I said to myself. I felt that little feeling of anger I sometimes felt in these kinds of moments. When I didn't understand something and someone else did. I pushed it down; it was silly to feel this way. He had offered to tell me, I was the one being stubborn now. I felt this need to prove that I knew the secret. Despite knowing the secret was a secret. That was kind of the purpose of secrets.

It didn't help that he was up a step, literally looking down at me, leaning so comfortably on the newel post.

Oh, of course.

I stepped up to join him and gave his elbow a quick shove. As he slipped off the post with a "Hey!" I examined it. There was a hinge on one side, clear as day now that I was looking for it. I pulled at the top of the post and it swung open. Inside was a copper button, extra shiny right in the middle. Right where clearly many a thumb had pushed on it.

So I pushed on it.

There was a loud clank and then a rusty whirring sound. I turned quickly to watch as the wall opposite us slowly opened. I approached and examined it. It wasn't cement after all. It was a heavy metal painted gray to match the rest of the walls.

"What purpose does this serve?" I asked. "A second secret entrance?"

"I assume this was where they made the hooch," replied Bill, joining me at the door. "They needed extra protections."

"I suppose so," I said, looking into the empty gray room beyond the door.

"There's more to go. Quite an adventure," said Bill as he walked into the room.

I followed him. I was feeling a little nervous now, not as excited as before. "Quite an adventure."

We passed quickly through the empty plain room. I imagined knowing what I knew now, that this room was used for storing goods before they were shipped out. We made our way to a large hole in the wall to our left and down yet another dark staircase. At the bottom we were greeted by a large room. I looked up and saw rusted baskets hanging from a line that ran around the room like a track for a model train set. Across from us were two giant tubs and, beside them, tables and overturned stools. The whole room felt ancient, like we had opened an Egyptian sarcophagus. Dust and ruin.

Except for the machine.

"Isn't it incredible?" Bill asked. "It's both terrifying and fascinating, don't you think?"

I wasn't sure about that. "What is it?" I asked, staring at it. It was quite the opposite of everything else in the room: new, shiny, but covered in some black spots here and there. It was completely modern and huge. Not at all like the old-fashioned bootlegger setups.

""""The time has come," the Walrus said, "to talk of many things . . ."""" replied Bill, walking toward it. I followed him.

"The Walrus?" I asked, feeling a little concerned. He was sounding weird now. Not giddy, not anxious, now he was sounding almost mesmerized. I noticed as he turned toward the machine a few more specks of black at the nape of his neck.

Black spots.

I glanced at the machine.

Bill placed a hand on it, almost like he was touching the side of a giant animal. He was deliberate and slow, drawing his hand across the side of the machine toward a massive opening on one side. He placed a hand on one of the large gears and pushed at it gently. I wasn't sure why, but nothing moved.

"From *Alice's Adventures in Wonderland*. Have you read the book?" he asked, still looking at the machine.

I didn't want to admit that I was not much of a reader of fiction. The only stories I knew were the ones my parents read to us from their giant worn copy of *The Complete Works of William Shakespeare*, which they did more for their own amusement than for ours. The books that interested me were the science ones. Or rather, I suppose, book. The one book I stole from school last year. I still believe I borrowed it. I knew someday I'd return it, once I had memorized it completely.

"I know of it," I replied. I was standing next to him now,

but I didn't want to touch the machine. Something about it made me uncomfortable.

"Well, it's a poem from the book. The Walrus and the Carpenter take several young oysters for a walk along the beach."

"Odd," I replied. Perhaps odder still was why on earth he was telling me any of this. Why was he acting so strange? It occurred to me then how dangerous innocuous strangeness could be. The beginning of our night together had been such fun, but now it had turned, like overripe fruit. I felt my defenses rise.

Bill gazed at the machine; he looked like he was almost in a trance. One could possibly say he was a man in love. But it was different somehow. Not love, but infatuation? Obsession, perhaps?

""The time has come," the Walrus said, "to talk of many things. Of shoes—and ships—and sealing-wax."" He turned the corner of the machine where a large pipe curved downward, opening up at the end. Bill bent down and stared up into the large gaping mouth. Almost stuck his entire head in. ""Of cabbages—and kings."" His voice echoed now a bit, and I took a small step backward. ""And why the sea is boiling hot—and whether pigs have wings."" He pulled his head out of the pipe, stood upright, and looked at me. "And what on earth is this thing for?"

"That's not part of your poem," I replied.

He shook his head. "You should look here, mad scientist. What is that black stuff?"

I suddenly didn't want to. I was feeling more and more concerned for Bill. Besides that, I was quite intimidated by the machine, and that giant opening looked like it might bite my head off if I stuck it inside. But I couldn't tell Bill that. I didn't want him to react badly, and at this point I really had no idea how he would.

I approached the mouth of the machine and bent my knees so I could look up inside it. It was completely black, like it had been painted. But it seemed wet. Like it had only just been. I wasn't keen on touching the stuff, but I assumed it was paint. Paint of a deep black color unlike any I had ever seen. A black so dark it felt like I was looking into a hole that fell down into the depths of the earth.

A hole, like Alice's from her book. I knew that much. She fell for forever and ended up in a completely new world. I felt a shudder rising in me. I didn't want to fall down any holes today.

I backed away and stood upright.

"It's paint. A very black paint."

"Like looking into a moonless sky," said Bill, agreeing.

I appreciated that he understood. "I've never seen anything like it."

"You should take a sample," he said. "For your chemistry set."

That spot deep inside me felt something different then, not fear or anger, but excitement. "I don't have a vial with me." I wished then that Bill had given me some time to prepare, not been quite so spontaneous with this visit.

"Then we'll come back with one." I could hear my excitement echo back at me in Bill's voice.

"What is this machine? What is it for, Bill?" I asked.

He shook his head. "I have no idea. I came here with Mr. Connor to help fix it. But what it does? No one told me. The Gent fellows have been so secretive. I thought maybe it was something to help with the plumbing at a large club, but the more I examine it, the more it looks like something that is meant to make something."

"Make something?"

"Don't you think so? There are no other tubes, there is no passage from one part to another. It's all self-contained. Except for this one exit." He indicated toward the pipe.

"Or entrance," I said.

Bill nodded. "Maybe." He paused. "It's a little funny."

"What is?" I slowly started to walk around the machine. My feet were taking control over my body, my curiosity was getting the better of me. *What are you?* I thought. And then I thought, *Why are you hidden?*

"Something Mr. Connor said. He talked about a monster. I thought it was a metaphor, but he seemed to imply it wasn't."

"You think they made a monster?" I asked. I was skeptical. When I arrived at the side Bill was standing by, I, too, placed a hand on the giant gear toward the bottom of the machine. I looked at Bill. He looked, well, for want of a better word, scared. "I don't think that's true," I said, trying to reassure him.

He shrugged and didn't say anything.

I ran my fingers over the teeth of the gear, up and down and up and down.

"How does the rest of the poem go?" I asked, trying to make him feel a bit better. I looked up at the machine. It rose so high when standing this close. It was overwhelming. There was a pipe here, large and winding toward the mouth of the machine like a boa constrictor.

"Oh, it just goes on and on, more absurdity, very typical," replied Bill, standing next to me and looking up as well.

"Of why the sea is 'boiling hot'?" But of course that's not true. Was that what absurdity was then? Just a lie? "What's the point of it?"

"They eat all the oysters," said Bill. He was looking closely at the pipe.

"I don't understand," I replied.

"They invite the little oysters for a walk and then eat them." He tapped on the pipe. It made a small hollow sound. He moved his hand up the pipe and tapped again. The same sound.

"That's the point of the poem?" Something about that horrified me.

"I don't know. But it's what happens."

Another tap. Another hollow sound.

"Oh," I said. "It's what happens."

23: BRANT

I caught the door just before it

slammed shut, my hand barricading it from closing fully. The sting ran up my arm, and I pressed my lips together firmly. I was not going to cry out. I knew I was close to blowing this whole story wide open. This would be my way onto the masthead. This would earn me that byline.

But boy, oh boy, did my hand hurt.

I pulled, my left hand joining my right as the door slowly, heavily slid open bit by bit. Voices floated up to me, Bill and Constance. I couldn't hear yet what they were saying.

I pulled at the door, my whole body straining at the effort. The thing must have been made of solid metal. Back in the days of Prohibition there was likely more than just the Anti-Saloon League and the police they wanted to keep out. This thing was bulletproof. And gang warfare was a common and bloody business.

There was a click. It was a heavy sound, like a decision had been made. I slowly relaxed my muscles still holding on to the side of the door. Then I quickly jumped through the open space into the room on the other side. I felt like a contortionist, still holding the door. I was not about to be crushed to death by some decades-old broken piece of hardware.

I let go then. The door stayed in place. I sighed and looked at my right hand. There was a deep gash running down the middle of my palm where I had grabbed at the serrated sides. I flexed my hand slightly; the sting was impressive. It radiated through my whole body. I thought about characters I'd read in books making blood oaths and slicing their palms to do so and found it absurd. Of all the places to cut yourself willingly? The palm? Really?

The voices were growing quieter and I realized I was losing track of Bill and Constance. I looked around the small gray cement room. It was completely empty, like a jail cell. But there was a gap in the wall, the width of a large man, with rough-hewn edges as if the thing had been made quickly once upon a time. I ran through and made my way down the narrow wooden stairs in the dark, tripping over my feet. I stumbled toward the bottom of the staircase, my heels missing its step, and I managed to arrive at the floor upright but shaken. That feeling of missing a step feels like you are stepping off the edge of a cliff, even if the next step is just a few inches down. My heart was pounding in my chest.

"You're Brant, right?" said Constance, and I looked up. She and Bill were standing in the distance beside a giant machine. It took up the entire other side of the room, and almost touched the ceiling. It was square with some curved pipes leading out and then back in again. And there was an opening to one side. The inside looked painted black. The whole thing looked relatively new; the metal gleamed. There was no sign of rust. But dark black stains followed the path of its seams. I couldn't tell from where I stood if it was some kind of mold possibly?

"Brant, old chum!" Bill looked shocked but not unhappy to see me. Almost relieved in fact.

I smiled tightly. I knew if I wanted the inside story, I needed to keep up the act, but being called "old chum" just felt, well, condescending.

"Hey, Bill! Sorry about the intrusion, pal." I laughed a bit. It wasn't like I had stumbled into his office or anything. Here we were, in the underbelly of Atlantic City, somewhere we had no right to be. I was hoping that fact would prevent Bill from any bigger questions, like, say, why I was here in the first place.

"Not an intrusion at all! In fact I'm glad you're here, I was showing Constance the machine. You'll probably get a kick out of it too." Something sounded off about Bill's voice. I just couldn't put my finger on it.

The machine.

I joined them and looked more closely at the thing. It was huge now that I was standing right next to it.

"What does it do?" I asked.

"Well, that's the question, isn't it?" replied Constance. "Something supersecret evidently."

"I'm not even supposed to know it's here," replied Bill.

"How did you find it?" I slowly started to walk around the machine, examining it closely from every angle. I arrived at the large opening at one side and peered into it. The black void stared back.

"I've been working with the Gent contractors."

I already knew this, of course—I'd been spying on him for weeks—but I turned to look at Bill and raised my eyebrows like it was a pleasant surprise. Then I looked back inside the machine, this time reaching up and touching the blackness. A sticky black residue covered my fingertips.

There was a sudden bang.

I jumped. My heart was racing fast from the shock, but instantly I felt ashamed for being such a coward. I turned to smile at the others even as I dried my sweaty palms on my trousers.

"What was that?" asked Bill.

"It sounded like it came from over there." Constance was pointing toward a large, white, rusted metal box, almost the height of the room, standing beside one of the sinks. A thick chain was wrapped around its middle like a belt.

"Looks like an old icebox," said Bill, approaching it.

I stayed where I was and watched the two of them examine the box for a moment. I turned back to the machine, to the black void. I stared at it hard. Had it been a coincidence that the loud jarring noise had happened when I'd touched the inside? I swallowed hard. But it wasn't fear anymore, it was an overwhelming excitement. I was so close to my story, to the truth. I felt elated.

"It's got a lock," said Constance.

"Looks new," Bill added just as I reached up inside the machine again. I felt this draw, a need to touch the blackness once more. Just to see . . . just to try.

My finger grazed the inside.

Bang.

Constance screamed.

I whipped around.

"Are you okay?" I asked. But I wasn't worried, I was excited. There was some kind of correlation, there had to be!

"There's something in there," she said, not turning to look at me. "There's something someone is keeping in there." She glanced over at Bill, who looked white as a sheet.

Then we need to know what it is, obviously, I thought to myself. I marched over to the icebox. "Okay then, let's see." I examined the chain and the lock. No rust, definitely new. This was it. This was the story, right here.

"I don't think we should open it," said Constance.

"We probably shouldn't," I replied with a grin. "That's why we're going to." I turned to look at Bill, to get him on my side. "Can you pick a lock, Mr. Fix-It?"

I knew he'd do it. I could see the indecision plain on his face, but I knew ultimately he'd do it. He was like me, curious about the world.

"Yes, I can." He approached the box tentatively.

"Wait," said Constance. I inwardly rolled my eyes. She marched over to the wall and picked up a bottle from the ground. She looked at it for a moment and then smashed it against the wall.

"Are you crazy?" I asked, staring at her.

She returned holding the broken bottle in her hand, the sharp edges sticking up like a demented torch.

"You two might want to encounter whatever it is unarmed, but I'm no fool," she replied, and held the bottle in front of her, staring hard at the icebox.

Okay, so maybe she wasn't so scared after all.

There was the sound of metal on metal as the chain suddenly slipped down the icebox. "It's done," said Bill, holding the lock and looking a little lost.

I grabbed the fallen chain and wrapped the end around my hand. Constance had a good idea there with the whole weapon thing.

"So, are we certain that we should open this door?" asked Constance.

"I am," I replied. I'd never felt more sure of anything in my life. "I'm going to try to jump whatever it is, so you should back away to the side," I told her.

She did, standing by Bill, his hand on the edge of the door.

"On three, you ready?" I asked.

"That's a complicated question," replied Bill.

I didn't have time for his convoluted way of talking. "One, two, three!"

24: BILL

I flung open the door as Brant stood in front, the chain in both his hands, ready to leap. I, for my part, was ready to grab Constance and run. I felt certain that whatever this monster was that Thomas was going on about, metaphor or not, human or . . . not, this was it. Right here in front of us. My hands were shaking.

There was a stillness that felt both welcome and not in that moment. There should have been a monster charging at us for all that noise coming from inside the icebox. But instead there was quiet.

"It's empty," said Constance, gripping her bottle tightly.

"It can't be," said Brant. He was standing right in front of the icebox. Right there staring into it. How could he doubt what his own eyes were telling him?

Then again, my own mind played tricks on me all the time.

I joined him at his side and looked into the box. It was indeed empty. Not even a black void like inside the machine. Just the back of an icebox. Rusted like its outside.

The world around us seemed to get darker, murkier, like we were being drawn into the thing. I shook my head, trying to make the world brighten. It was my mind playing tricks on me again. I hated I had so little control over it.

"Did a light just go out?" asked Constance, her voice turning into a whisper.

My heart leapt into my throat. It wasn't just me then, a figment of my imagination? It was real? I looked around. The lights still buzzed overhead. But she was right. It really seemed darker in the room. Why? What was happening? I felt the urge to run, but I calmed myself down. There had to be a logical explanation, there was no room for panic. Not yet.

"The shadows," she whispered, and pointed at the wall.

"Well, that's strange," said Brant, finally speaking up, sounding as confident as ever. "What do you think makes a thing like that happen?"

Black shadows seemed to drip down the walls while others oozed out from the floor to meet them. We seemed to be at some kind of gruesome center, where all the shadows were aiming to meet.

How could Brant be this calm?

Constance stepped forward toward the shadows and bent down to look closer. This was wrong. This was so very wrong.

"We should leave," I said. Dread crawled over my skin.

"Don't you want to know what's happening?" asked Brant.

"No."

I did not. I wanted to leave. We all needed to leave.

"There's nothing there," said Constance, returning to our little group, speaking quietly but urgently. Her eyes were wide with concern. "It's nothing tangible. It's just a shadow."

"A shadow of what?" I asked, watching as it seeped closer, noticing as it did the room was growing darker and darker.

"I don't know," she replied. Her voice quivered as her eyes looked about the room.

We stood there, frozen to the spot, not by any outside force but by the weight of our own fears and confusion. At least . . . at least I did. The room got darker and darker.

And darker.

It seeped around us. At any moment it would seep into us. I felt drawn to it even as I was repelled by it. We needed to move. We needed to move now.

We stayed still.

"You know what," said Brant, suddenly a lot closer to me than he was a moment ago, his voice finally tinged with concern, "you're right. We should leave."

That's when the lights went out.

There was no fuse box to find this time. There was no reasonable solution to the darkness. No wires to connect. It was a kind of darkness you only see when you close your eyes.

A piercing scream. Constance.

Then I was whipped onto the floor. My body slammed into the cold stone hard, but the searing pain I felt was something else. Something had grabbed my foot and was dragging me, something sharp was digging into my ankle. I wanted to

scream from the pain but my fight-or-flight response took hold
and adrenaline filled my body. I turned around onto my back and
kicked with my free foot. I kicked straight down at whatever it
was. My foot connected with something solid. There was something there, something real, something that wasn't just in my
head. I yelled loudly as I kicked again with all my strength.
There was an otherworldly, piercing scream that sounded like a
roar. I kicked at it again and again, heart beating furiously. The
sharpness scraped down my foot, causing me to cry out in pain,
but I was free and scrambling up, being pulled by the back of my
shirt by someone above me.

I was on my feet, my ankle stinging hard, and Brant said,
panting, "Are you okay?"

"Let's get out of here, boys, now!" Constance yelled.

I whipped my head around and found her. She was over by
the exit, dirt on her face, her dress torn at the shoulder, and
I realized then that I could see her. The blackness around her
was retreating. The shadows were slipping deeper and deeper
into the room, where Brant and I stood, leaving light on the
fringes.

There was a sudden crash and I turned around. It was hard
to see into the depths of the dark, but with the little light from
our escape route I saw a large, hulking shadow of something
that looked like it was attacking the machine. It ran into it,
like a charging bull, but the machine was solid and stayed put.

A monster. Not a metaphor. A real monster. I could taste
bile in my throat, my head burned from the fear.

"Bill! Now!"

I felt Brant pulling on my shoulder, but I was drawn to the show in front of me. What was this monster? It looked tall and wiry, like a shadow itself, but its head was huge. It thrashed at the machine with claws that glinted in the light. Suddenly the machine came to life, lighting up the surrounding area with a sickly yellow glow.

Large teeth reflected in the illumination.

Like a dream coming to life.

A nightmare coming to life.

The machine sputtered and cranked to life like a beast of another kind. And then began vomiting all over the ground, right where we had been standing. Out of the giant open pipe came a thick black liquid. It poured out, quickly flowing into all corners of the room. The demon roared again.

"Bill!" This time it was Constance, and hearing her voice so loud and so angry, I was jolted back to reality.

I turned and ran toward her, with Brant close behind.

We ran for the exit and up the stairs, the sound of the roar still echoing in my ears, mixing with the sound of my blood rushing in my head and my heart racing. It was a cacophony of noise. The pain in my foot snaked its way up my leg like a lightning strike. I heard another roar from behind us and it made me take the stairs two at a time, sweat now dripping down my forehead. I looked back and saw the shadows chasing us, climbing up the walls like vines. The black goo was floating at the bottom of the stairs, slowly rising. If we weren't eaten alive by this beast, then we might very well drown.

The secret door was closed at the top of the steps, but I knew how to open it. There was a small button hidden in the shadow of the corner. I'd seen Mr. Connor push it on our way out. I reached out with my shaking hand and pushed it. I heard the gears grinding. It sounded off, something was wrong.

"This isn't right," I said, more to myself than anything. I fiercely shoved aside my rising panic to focus on solving the problem. I wiped the sweat from my brow.

"I had to wrench it open to follow you," said Brant, panting at my side. "That might have done something."

I looked at him, but could only see him faintly in the shadowy dark. There was no time to point fingers, but I really wanted to. Why would he do this to us? What was he thinking? I turned back to the button, and felt around it. There had to be a panel of some kind.

"It's rising," said Constance, a desperate edge to her voice.

"I know," I replied, trying to stay calm but trembling all the same.

I got on my knees and traced my hand over the wall all the way down to the floor, trying to feel for anything, anything at all. There had to be something . . . something . . .

My finger caught on a divot and I pushed. A panel moved under my hand and I quickly removed it. My eyes were adjusting to the dark, but the dark was leeching more and more light from the air. I couldn't see. I just went for it and reached my hand into the small hole in the dark. I felt around and came to a lever. My heart stopped and I remembered earlier, a similar lever, a spray of black wet. I could do this, I had to do this. I pulled down hard. More grinding sounds, and then a clang.

"It's opening!" said Constance.

"I've got it," added Brant.

I stood up to see the door open just enough to fit a single body through, Brant straining to keep it that wide in the first place.

"Constance, go," he ordered, and she looked at both of us before slipping through.

"I can help," she said from the other side, her gloved hands appearing around the edge of the door, pulling at it from her side.

"Bill, come on," said Brant, his voice now straining with the effort.

I just stared at him, and then at the door. I heard the gears grinding, I could even smell the friction of metal on metal. The thought of the door slamming shut, slamming into a body. Crushing it.

"Bill!"

I found myself through the door. Just like so many other moments I've lost in my mind. I was just there.

"Bill!"

But this time it was Constance. She was still attempting to brace the door open with Brant. I immediately joined her, grabbing hard while the door pushed back with all its might against us. We weren't strong enough for this. It was only thanks to the grace of some gears the door was open this much at all.

"Brant, you have to jump through," said Constance, her voice strained.

"You have to do it now," I added. The smell of burning filled the air.

Brant took in a deep breath and nodded.

I felt the door pushing into my hands hard now. I heard another clang, and suddenly there was a sickening weight against my palms. Constance cried out but didn't let go. He had to do it now.

Brant jumped.

There was a loud clank and I instinctively grabbed Constance and pulled her away as the door mechanism took control. We fell onto the ground, and I stayed there for a moment, panting hard, feeling the sting in my palms, and in my ankle.

"Brant!"

I sat up and turned to see Constance on the ground, pulling at Brant by the door. I stood and scrambled over, and then stopped at the scene before me. Brant's torso stuck out through the door, his bottom half trapped on the other side. The door was crushing him. If we didn't do something, if we didn't help him . . .

"Constance, stop," he said, wheezing.

The landing was brightly lit. Being able to see so clearly almost felt like too much. But it made finding the opposite panel much easier on this side and I could even see what was behind it.

I found the same lever, but it was loose to the touch; moving it did nothing. I looked past it, farther into the darkness of the wall, and saw a large brass button with "Stop/Start" on it. I hit it with all my might.

The grinding stopped. The smell of metal on metal lingered in the air.

I felt my body go limp with relief.

"Brant, stay with us!" cried Constance.

Please, Brant, stay with us.

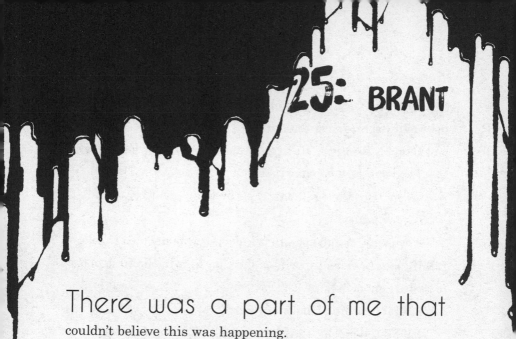

25: BRANT

There was a part of me that couldn't believe this was happening.

Then there was the part of me that was in a lot of pain.

Pain.

Intense terrible pain.

And a terrible, terrible understanding. I stared at Constance's hands in her white kid gloves. Feeling her pull my arms, and the desperation in that moment. I couldn't make eye contact.

"Brant!"

I couldn't think to describe the sensation. The tightness around my torso, crushing the air out of me. Feeling like at any moment I might burst like a balloon. And the sharp stabbing pain in my middle.

But then there were my legs, the growing wetness up from my ankles, like I was slowly slipping into the ocean. It was so cold, shockingly cold. It shouldn't be that cold. I didn't understand. Until suddenly, I understood. The black ooze. It was still rising from the basement. Still making its slow but steady journey. As it climbed up my legs, I felt it tighten around them and start to pull me back. Back toward the darkness and that thing. Constance pulled on my arms; the sticky inky black liquid pulled at my legs.

They will pull me apart.

"Stop." But the word barely escaped my mouth.

It's my fault.

It was my idea to open that icebox. It was my idea to follow Bill. It was my idea to write a story on him in the first place. It was all my own fault.

It's kind of funny, but not really.

It's all too much. It's time to give in. To stop fighting.

I felt okay with this decision. I felt light-headed like I was drunk and perfectly okay with this decision. I could now make eye contact.

We did. She was staring at me wide-eyed, tears streaming down her face. She'd probably never seen death before, or if she had she'd never held it by the hand.

I smiled. I wanted her to know I was okay.

It's fine.

My only regret was I never wrote any of it down. None of it. No notes, just kept it all in my head like I always did.

"Brant! Stay with us!"

Why did I never write any of it down?

I should have written it down.

26: CONSTANCE

Brant went limp. I instantly felt for a pulse on his wrist, tears in my eyes. I knew this was something you could do. I'd read it in my old science book. Be alive, Brant, please be alive. You have to be alive. His skin was slick with sweat as I felt around his wrist. There it was, faint, but it was there. I felt a relief and then an instant sense of urgency.

"Come on, Bill, we have to pull," I said, keeping all my focus on Brant's limp body.

"We can't do anything for him here. He's trapped. Even if we were strong enough, we'd pull him apart, not to safety," he replied.

"Then open the door, make it work, make the door work." That's what you're good at, Bill, make it work. I was desperate but I was also right. I had to be right.

"I can't," he said softly.

"Then go get help." I finally turned to look at him sitting across the landing from me, and he stared at me with this expression I didn't understand. He looked almost like he was in a trance, but it wasn't that. He was just scared.

"We can't," he said.

"Of course you can!" This was ridiculous!

Bill looked down and closed his eyes, then opened them again. "This is our fault. Don't you see? There's something secret down there, something we were never supposed to know about."

"It doesn't matter, we can deal with that after. Just get someone, anyone."

I turned back to Brant. I couldn't let go of his hands.

This couldn't really be it, could it? This wasn't it. A day couldn't start so lovely and simple and end in this way. It just couldn't.

I could sense Bill move and get up. He was standing beside me. He was using a different tactic, I guessed. It infuriated me. "Constance, we have to leave. You have to let go of him. He wouldn't want you to hold on like this. He wouldn't want you to have to bear the burden of his mistakes."

"I don't know what he would have wanted. We barely knew each other." I stared at the body of the young man in front of me, limp on the ground. He was still here, he could still be saved.

"Well, I knew him and you have to believe me."

I looked at him again. I'd never seen Bill like this, all disheveled, a blotchy red face, hair out of place. He was terrified. I was too. Of course I was. But I couldn't just leave Brant. I couldn't. Even if he would have preferred it that way. People don't always make the right decisions for themselves or others. His life was worth that risk.

I turned back to Brant. I needed a sign telling me what to do. Do I let go or not? Could I even let go? Could I ever let go?

It was then I noticed the inky black liquid spreading up over his torso. The ooze. From downstairs. It had found its way up to us. To him. I inhaled sharply.

Then a thought passed over me. I hadn't really taken a good look at the substance yet. I was horrified but fascinated. I leaned closer to look at it carefully. It was so thick, it looked sticky, and it seemed to grow up Brant's body in branches, reaching and clawing its way up like fingers. I couldn't understand what liquid would work that way, that it didn't ooze and flow; instead it had sharp edges and points.

"Constance, we have to go now." Bill put his hand on mine, trying to physically pry my fingers off Brant's.

"What *is* it?" I asked. I leaned in and over Brant's body even farther. The ooze was up to his shoulders now, enveloping his torso in thick blackness, dripping on the floor beneath him.

"It's that black stuff, from downstairs," replied Bill, pulling at my hand harder. He was no longer suggesting I let go, he was basically forcing me to. I didn't like that. I didn't like that at all.

"I know that," I replied, snapping at him. He recoiled as I stared him down, and removed his hand from mine. I'd never snapped like that before. I calmed myself down to explain. "But what is it made of? Why is it behaving like this?"

"Constance, this isn't the time for analysis."

He wasn't wrong. But I just couldn't let go of Brant. Of this need to know. Of any of it. Something inside me was twisting in a way I didn't understand. I stared as the ink climbed up Brant's neck toward his head.

"Bill, it's going to drown him. We need to get him out now!" I pulled so hard now but it was so stupidly futile. I watched, horrified, as the ooze poured and clawed its way over the side of his head. As it sank into his ear, as it spilled over his closed eyes, his nose, into his slack mouth, until his face was gone and just an inky shadow remained. And still the ink defied all reasonable behavior and snaked its way along his arms, pulling at them as it moved toward his hands, my hands. I felt sick. I was beyond fear now, I was somewhere else. Somewhere that hollowed out my body, made my skin feel like paper, my eyes sink deep into my skull. I felt aware of myself as a shell holding in blood and bone. I didn't feel human. I looked at my hands holding Brant's hands. They were there. They were real. I was real. I existed.

And then Bill was pulling on me, on my shoulders. I looked up at him. All his manners and over-the-top gentlemanliness thrown to the side to get me to just let go. There was something about that I liked. The veneer never seemed sincere.

That rhymed.

I giggled to myself. I felt like how it must feel to have one too many glasses of champagne. A strange light-headed feeling. Brant's hands squeezed mine and I flinched, shocked at the sudden movement. He was awake?

I looked down at my hands. The inky black liquid was climbing up them. I realized that it wasn't Brant squeezing me, it was the strange substance. It was tightening my grip, pinching my hands tight inside the gloves. For the first time the urgency to let him go surged through me. I started to pull away, to pull my hands out of Brant's. But they were stuck together, fused together like melted metal.

"I can't let go," I said. Bill still had me by the shoulders.

"You have to," he replied.

"No, I mean I'm stuck; I'm stuck to him." I pulled harder, the panic rising as the black goo made its way over my fingers and up my hand. I was pulling so hard now I was swinging both my arms and Brant's, like I was puppeting some demon marionette.

"Let me pry his fingers off," said Bill, coming around to beside our arms.

"No!" I said it with such force I was surprised.

"What?"

"No, if you touch the substance, if you touch it . . ." I didn't know what the rest of the sentence was but I knew I was right. I thought about Bill and the black specks on his face, about his strange draw to the machine. About all of it. "No, let me do this. It's the gloves. If I can just . . ."

The ooze made it hard to relax my fingers within Brant's grasp but I was able to wiggle them a little. The black substance ran up to my wrist, toward the edge of my gloves.

"How can I help?" asked Bill.

"I don't know."

He reached over me and grabbed at both my forearms, taking them gently in his hands, and started to pull, not hard, not so it hurt, but to help, I supposed. I wasn't sure it was really all that helpful, but I let him.

I felt the gloves slip down my fingers, catching at the tip. The top of my hands were free, but the ink quickly grabbed hold. I pulled hard now, not caring if I tore my own skin away. I was frantic.

"Pull!" I ordered. Bill pulled lightly at my forearms, his fingers grazing my skin like he was petting a skittish cat. Anger was rising up inside me. Why was he so completely useless?

"Pull, damn it!" I yelled. My voice was sharp, but I kind of liked it. I felt the anger in my chest as I pulled as well.

Bill clearly took me seriously and finally grabbed my arms tightly, almost to the point of cutting off my circulation, and pulled. We synched our actions and pulled and pulled. The tips of my fingers stung as the gloves ripped away from my skin.

Then with great momentum and in complete shock we flew backward, my fingers free of my gloves. In the same instance, the black goo exploded, and I raised my arms instinctively to protect my face. Droplets rained everywhere, and when finally there was stillness, I looked up to see what had happened.

Before me, where Brant's body had been, covered in the black, was a seeping puddle. There was no sign of Brant, his form, his presence, nothing. Just a puddle that seemed to reach out toward me and Bill until suddenly the heavy metal door slammed shut.

I screamed, and held up my arms once more. Then when I realized what had happened, I lowered them and stared at the small inky puddle before us. It started to sink backward, toward the closed metal door, sneaking away from us, slipping through the cracks.

Then it was gone.

He was gone.

Brant was gone.

"Are you okay?" asked Bill.

What a question to ask; of course I wasn't okay. But I knew he meant if I was okay physically. I supposed aside from my stinging fingers, I was. "Yes." I brought my hands up close and looked at them. The fingertips were red and raw, and there was black at my wrists where the ink had seeped under the edge of my gloves. I noticed then the black on my sleeves and looked down at my skirt. More black droplets from the explosion. I turned and looked at Bill. He had more black speckles on his face and some now in his hair. "How about you?"

"I'm okay." He didn't look okay. "Come on, let's get out of here."

He was right. It was time. The idea of just leaving felt overwhelming but it was the only thing to do. We were tangled together so it took a moment for us to help each other to standing. I stared at Bill. The ink was splattered across his body from head to toe and I assumed I must look the same. He looked down at himself. "Well, my father's going to kill me."

The anger welled up inside me again, like a sudden explosion of light in the darkness. "At least that's just a metaphor. At least you aren't Brant."

Bill looked at me. There was a look of betrayal in his eyes, and I immediately felt guilty.

"I'm sorry," I said quietly, looking down. "I'm just upset."

"I am too," he replied, also quietly. We stood there in silence and then when not quite enough time had passed, he said, "We have to get out of here."

He was right, I knew he was right. Brant had just been exploded into goop, and here we were, the only two people around. We would be blamed for it all.

Then again. Was it not in a way our fault? Should we not be blamed?

I looked at the small black stain on the floor, and my mind just couldn't fully wrap itself around the idea that Brant had vanished like that. That he had been, and now he wasn't. I wanted to cry but it was all too unbelievable.

All I felt was guilt. And a burning ember of anger.

"Let's go." I bent down and picked up my gloves carefully, pinching them from the inside. They were coated in black but I couldn't just leave them there. Evidence.

Evidence.

Of a crime.

What had we done?

27: BILL

The house felt dead. Not that

that ought to have been a surprise. Houses were built from dead materials after all: dead trees, dried earth, muddy water. And they were built on dead land, killing everything beneath it, purposeful destruction, the removing of life. Digging up roots. Tossing away mountains of grass.

But homes, homes had souls. A hearth. Warmth and laughter. Homes had personalities that you could feel the moment you entered them.

My home felt dead.

Maybe it had always felt dead. There had never been a love between me and this building, that was for certain. But as I entered the foyer and closed the front door quietly behind me, I felt a cold, empty feeling. Like I had entered a mausoleum.

Then I was in my room. Time had slipped again, and I was standing there, in my drawers, my ink-stained clothes in a heap on the floor beside me. I felt numb, and a little stupid. Like any thought I needed to unravel couldn't penetrate my thick skull. The term "combat fatigue" circled my head for a moment. My father had spoken about it. Not for himself, obviously. He had never served. I had no idea how he'd managed to get around the draft, but he had. Dodged it as easily as any questions about how he had managed it. But he still spoke of the war as if he'd had firsthand experience. So much so that maybe some believed he had it. Maybe he now believed he had, too. Saying something over and over can make you believe it.

Brant isn't dead.

Brant isn't dead.

Brant isn't dead.

"Combat fatigue," my father had said, "was a made-up term for people who had no backbone."

That couldn't be true. Not after the war. I found myself on the floor, curled into the fetal position, nothing holding me upright. Nothing able to hold me upright. No bones. No muscles. No will. I felt empty, severely empty. Hollow. Like a husk. The lack of something was overwhelming any other feelings. I felt like I was inside out.

I felt.

I felt.

Brant had just burst like a bubble. One moment he was there and the next he was a puddle.

I felt.

This gnawing fear began to fill the empty pockets inside me. It overwhelmed everything, flooding over me like that sticky black ooze enveloped Brant. I couldn't escape it. I closed my eyes and all I saw was Brant's body bursting. I opened them and all I saw were four corners of a room that couldn't protect me. Nothing could protect me. I needed to escape; I needed out.

I was on my feet, my backbone working again, it seemed. And then I was in my father's study, at his bar filled with crystal decanters that glinted in the light of something somewhere outside. Men have drunk themselves to death, they say. I'd never seen it. But I didn't need death, I just needed a bit of fake death right now. I had seen my father asleep on the settee in the formal sitting room facedown in a puddle of his drool enough times to see how alcohol could simulate a fake death.

I needed to black out. I needed to force my mind to skip time. Why did it always jump and land in a moment when my brain was most furious, when my feelings were most raw? Why couldn't I skip those parts?

I picked up a decanter of whiskey, the crystal container heavy in my hand. How did this work? Did I just drink it all? Like Alice's potion? Would it make me small, so small, smaller than the dust particles in the air? Would I disappear?

Brant exploding into a puddle of goo.

"Mr. Chambers?"

I turned. Anna, the housekeeper, was standing in her bathrobe, her long braid over one shoulder. She stared at me and for a moment I was in her place. Looking at a pale child in his underwear holding a large decanter of whiskey in his hand like a bottle of milk.

"I'm fine, Anna. Go back to sleep," I said.

She continued to stare at me. My words did not match anything happening in this room at the moment. Why would she trust them? But she slowly turned and did what she was told and left. I missed Mrs. Walker. She would have pushed the issue. She would have grabbed the decanter and marched me upstairs. Forced me into my pajamas. Ordered me to sleep. The best housekeeper in the world. The best mother a boy could have if he didn't have a mother.

I put down the decanter. This was absurd. I didn't like drinking in the first place. There was a much simpler way, I realized. To skip time. To fall unconscious.

I walked across the office to the wall and bashed my head against it.

Pain exploded through my body, stars sparked in my vision, but I was still conscious to feel it.

Darn.

So I bashed my head against the wall again.

I don't remember anything after that.

28: CONSTANCE

When I was a child, our neighbor had a little white-and-black terrier named Spot. He barked too much and ran into our apartment whenever Mother accidentally left the door open.

"Out, damned Spot!" she'd say with a grin, and it wasn't until I was older and we three girls were sitting on Mother's bed as she read from her complete works of William Shakespeare that I learned it was a very famous line from a very famous play. The character was crazy, and saw spots of blood where there weren't any. She tried furiously to wash them away. But she couldn't.

What they don't tell you is that blood is much easier to get out than ink.

I tried to imagine Spot the dog as I washed my dress in the tub. I sat there on my knees, in my nightgown, furiously scrubbing. I tried to imagine Spot the dog in the doorway and telling him to get out, out now, please, leave. You little rascal. But my imagination was not strong enough. My hands were still stained black, and my efforts to wash my dress clean were proving very much in vain.

I scrubbed and I scrubbed, and the more I tried, the angrier I got. The feeling just wouldn't stay down, the guilt was still there, oh yes, but it was holding the gate open now, enjoying watching the flow of rage fill and overtake me. I'd never felt anything like this before, and I couldn't even take a moment to notice it. That is, until the dress tore in my hands, not even at the seam, but at the skirt. A giant frayed hole stared up at me.

I leaned back on my heels and, with the wet back of my hand, brushed the hair that had fallen across my face. It was then that I noticed my breath rushing to catch up with me. Like I'd run a race.

Had I run? Had I run home?

Or was it just the ink on my dress and my madness trying to clean it.

"I think I ran home," I said out loud.

My voice sounded thin and too quiet, even for me. That made the anger in my gut bubble up again.

"No!" I said to it. Louder this time. I felt a strange elation at the sound of my voice echoing in our small bathroom. I smiled to myself and looked back at the dress. It was ruined now. Mother would be angry.

But since it was ruined . . .

I pulled the wet fabric out of the tub and dragged the dress out of the bathroom and into my own room. I knew somewhere inside that the water was trailing behind me, but I felt like I was walking in a dream.

I sat on my little chair and put the wet mass of dress on my desk. It flopped onto it like a large dead fish. I looked around quickly for something to cut the material with, if I had the sewing kit in my room . . . but then I realized, who needs scissors?

I grabbed the fabric and pulled, the sound of the tearing more pronounced now that it wasn't underwater. It was so satisfying. I pulled at the frayed edges, the muscles in my arms and neck tight and engaged. When the piece of fabric came free from the rest of the dress, I felt that same elated feeling and smiled. My anger was almost turning joyful.

I got up and then bent down onto my knees, reaching under my bed. My hand touched the edge of the box of my chemistry set and my fingers grabbed for it. I pulled it out and sat admiring it for a moment, gently caressing the cover. It was such a beautiful object. I opened it. It unfolded into my lap, three separate sections with bottles tightly fixed to the cardboard backing. It all looked so perfect; I didn't even want to use it.

But of course I did want to use it.

I unhooked the dropper from its little holder and then reached for the tiny bottle of bleach. That's where I'd start, in the obvious place. I quickly filled up the dropper.

I carefully held it just above the ink. My hand was shaking a little, and I reached up with the other one to adjust my goggles, to make sure they were tight around my eyes. I didn't know what kind of reaction this strange substance might produce, if it might be a noxious gas even. With that in mind . . .

I held my breath as I squeezed the dropper. A single drop fell onto the surface of the fabric, onto the ink. But the ink did not mingle or evaporate or do anything that I could have predicted. Instead it peeled itself away from the drop and moved around it, circling it. I leaned even closer, still not breathing. The drop was so small but my eyesight was keen. Was the ink . . . was it climbing up the sides of the little drop?

I tapped the drop with the dropper to burst it. It didn't spread like a bubble, but instead raced this way and that as if it was trying to escape. To escape the ink on all sides.

Brant's inky body exploded in my mind's eye.

I sat upright. I yanked the goggles off and felt my throat constrict. I stared down at my hands, still stained.

29: BILL

I woke up in bed, in my night-clothes, to a sunbeam directly across my face. I squinted and felt my whole body ache. My ankle was stinging in pain, reminding me of its damage by a steady throbbing in tune with my heartbeat. I tried to prop myself upright.

What had happened? Had time slipped away from me again? I reached up to run my fingers through my hair and felt some fabric at my forehead. I touched it and flinched.

A bandage on my head. Had I fallen down at some point?

There was a light tapping at my door.

"Yes?" I called out, still hazy and disoriented.

"Sir, there's a young lady to see you. I tried to send her away but she's rather insistent."

"Yes, please send her away. Thank you, Anna," I said, leaning against my headboard. Then: "Wait. What's her name?"

"It's a Miss Constance Gray."

Everything came flooding back to me then in such a rush that I turned quickly to the side of my bed, bent over, and threw up. I stared at the puddle of vomit and flashed to the inky one from the night before, the remains of Brant now an inky nothing. I fell back onto my bed with the taste of sick in my mouth and the pain in my head throbbing.

"Mr. Chambers?"

"Tell her . . . tell her I'll be down momentarily. I need to freshen up."

"Yes, sir."

What was she doing here? How had she found me? I felt fear wash over me again, and remembered the acute need to run away from it. Run away from everything. I remembered my father's study. The crystal decanters. The wall. I lightly touched my forehead. What a mad thing to do. Yet it had worked. A dreamless sleep, passing almost too quickly. One night was not enough. I needed to sleep for days. For months.

Constance. Constance who'd held Brant by the hand. Who'd witnessed his explosion, too. She was downstairs, likely seeking solace and comfort after what we'd been through. It didn't assuage my fear, but it did motivate me to throw the covers off my bed in one swoop and then finally rise to standing.

In the pool of my own vomit.

Wonderful.

"Constance!" I said a little too loudly as I entered the sitting room. Partly I was trying to hide my level of discomfort, partly it was the discovery that she wasn't alone. My father, of all people, was keeping her company, sitting in his large dark red wing chair while she very daintily sipped a glass of water on the sofa by the window.

"What happened to your head?" he asked immediately.

Well, that answered that question. My mysterious nurse had to have been Anna then. *Why would it have been Father at all?* I thought to myself, feeling a little stupid I had considered it.

"I'm fine," I replied as Constance stood and I took her hand. "Constance, it's lovely to see you."

She nodded. "You too." For all we had been through the night before, she seemed quite, well, normal, for want of a better word. Her hair was perfectly curled, her jacket and dress, plain but neat and clean. Not a trace of ink anywhere on her person.

"Father, may we have some privacy?" I asked, not sure if he'd give it to us.

He sat for a moment and then finally stood. "Of course. Lovely to see you again, Miss Gray." He turned to me as he passed and said, not remotely quietly, "She's lovely and very pretty. Have your fun with her but she's not the one."

I wanted to run away, what a thing to say.

"That was incredibly rude of you," said Constance.

I glanced at my father, whose face had turned red. I turned to look at Constance, who had put her hand over her mouth, her eyes wide with shock. "I'm so sorry, sir," she said.

"Who do you think you are?" asked my father.

I felt rooted to the spot, unable to think or do anything.

"I am so sorry," she said again.

"Get out of my house!" he ordered, pointing hard at the front door. Constance nodded and stood immediately, keeping her eyes lowered as she passed by me and my father. "I know of your sisters, girl. I've seen them out on the town with a different suitor every night. You're just like them, aren't you, trying to lure some rich man to marry you?"

Constance said nothing, but I saw her hand trembling as she reached out for the doorknob.

"Then there's you, on the diving platform, in your bathing costume in front of hundreds, no modesty. No shame."

She turned around and stared down my father. "Then what do we call the man who hired her?"

She turned and threw open the door and stormed out of the house.

"If I ever see you in my home again . . . !" called my father after her through the open door, then slammed it behind him. His rage was absolute but there was something in it that felt weak. Small. Especially compared with Constance's. Hers had a strange power behind it I'd never seen before.

Meanwhile all I was feeling was a great shame; I was feeling more than enough shame for everyone in the room. In the whole street. I stared at the formidable door in front of me as I heard my father storm off into his study.

And then I found I could move again. It was my turn to fling the door open.

"Constance!" I ran down the walk and turned to catch up to her running down the street. She was fast. I reached out to grab her shoulder but she stopped short and turned. Her face was fire.

"How dare he?! I saved him and his little film. How dare he talk like that about a person? Any person!" She made to move past me back toward the house but I blocked her. Now I was no longer scared for myself, but for her.

"He was wrong. Everything he said was wrong and you were right. But you cannot confront him. You don't understand just how dangerous he can be."

Her eyes were wild. She paced in front of me like a caged animal.

"After everything we've been through, I'm not scared of men like him anymore," she said.

I didn't know what to say to that but I did know we needed to talk. We needed to talk about everything.

"Come with me," I said. "There's a small park around the corner where we can talk."

She looked at me, still seething, and, then, finally, nodded.

I led her down the street and around the corner to the park. It was so small, really just a plot of land, not big enough for a home in this neighborhood. But it had a fine oak tree and a nice little white painted bench under it. It all looked a little bare this time of year, but it was a nice enough place to discuss monsters in the dark.

"How are you?" I asked as we sat.

"I'm fine," she replied, looking down and playing with a loose thread on her coat.

"No, not like that. How *are* you?" She didn't say anything. I realized then I needed to take the lead. I could share with her for some reason. Just like I'd shared the machine with her in the first place. I still trusted her that way. "I'm not well," I admitted. "I'm scared. I'm scared through and through. I don't understand what happened. It's like it was a nightmare."

"But it wasn't," she said quietly.

"No."

We sat for a moment as a cold breeze blew through the oak tree, its arms creaking in the wind, its fingers reaching out for something intangible.

"Are you sad?" asked Constance then.

"Sad?"

"About Brant. I . . . I think I feel sad about it. But I mostly feel very angry. I also didn't know him very well so maybe that's why?" She stopped and closed her eyes. Then she opened them and looked at me. They were so blue. I couldn't find any comparison to describe how blue they were. They were just so very blue. "I think I'm a bad person."

"You're not," I said, instinctively grabbing at her hands. She let me take them.

"We need to tell someone," she said. "Maybe one of those Gent people? They need to know something is down there, they need to know about the ink . . ."

I shook my head. I felt the fear rising in my throat again. "Absolutely not."

"Bill!"

"Absolutely not, Constance! Whatever it was, Gent knows about it. Otherwise why was it locked up? And the ink? That came from inside their machine. Gent knows everything."

"Then we have to stop them! We have to before someone else . . ."

Again I shook my head. Didn't she understand that this was not how it worked? She hadn't lived in my world. Any company that could afford such a machine, that could hide it, that had such dark huge secrets, they had to be protected by something huge as well.

"It's too dangerous," I said.

At that she laughed. "More dangerous than last night? I want to do this, Bill. I need to do this . . ."

"And does it matter what I want?" I asked her.

"What *do* you want, Bill?" She was looking at me now with that fierceness from before. It was something I'd found so attractive about her yesterday. But now I was seeing the dark side of it. The side that spoke to unpredictable behavior. I couldn't handle it.

"I want to forget any of it happened. I want to move on, and agree that we will take this secret to our graves."

Constance looked at me for a moment. I couldn't tell what she was thinking, but I could tell that there was a whirlwind swirling inside her.

"I hear you, Bill," she said, surprisingly calm, ending the long silence. "Let's move on. We can't allow one night to consume us forever."

She was quiet then, and still. I squeezed her hand. She didn't squeeze it back. Instead she let go and sighed gently. I watched as she stood up slowly, smoothing the front of her coat and then reaching behind to make sure it fell down her back properly. All of it seemed unconscious, habit, the small things we do every day. "I should go."

And she left without saying good-bye or even turning to look at me. I watched as she went, no longer a whirl of fury. But something else. Something that concerned me even more. Something more contained and focused. Like a bullet.

The fear returned.

There was no way she was going to move on.

It had been a lie. To make me feel better, I supposed. But it was still a lie.

And I had no idea what she was going to do next.

CONSTANCE

"You're not eating," said Andrew, pointing out the obvious. He had a way of doing that. "You forgot your hat," "The sky is very blue today." It was sweet but also incredibly dull. I appreciated his concern for me, I suppose, but it was funny. My lack of hunger at a high tea was not at the top of my list of concerns.

"What do you know about monsters?" I asked, picking up a sandwich from the three-tiered serving dish between us and placing it on my little plate with the painted flowers curling around its edges.

Andrew laughed a little. "Monsters? As in storybook monsters? Ogres, trolls, that sort of creature?"

I shook my head. That wasn't what I meant. But I also didn't know what I meant. "No, I mean in real life."

"Metaphorical monsters then? Like murderers? Like the Nazis during the war?" He took a sip of tea and looked at me, amused, over the edge of the cup.

"No, not like that either." I was getting frustrated. There was no reason to be so annoyed with him. He didn't understand. He would never understand. Just like Bill didn't understand. Just like no one would ever understand.

"Hey now, you're looking so serious. Are you okay?" asked Andrew, putting down the teacup and reaching across the table for my hand. I gave it to him to hold. "No gloves?" he asked.

My stomach clenched. "Is that a problem?"

"No! I love being able to hold your hand. You are always so put together though. It's a nice change." He smiled at me.

My gloves. My gloves caked in ink were sitting at home on my desk. I didn't know what to do with them. I couldn't figure out what properties the ink had so they seemed useless to keep. But I feared throwing them away. What if they were found? What if the ink contaminated other things?

"Do you think monsters could exist? Dinosaurs existed. They are like monsters in some way. Is it possible that strange shadowy monsters, like the ones they say live in your closet . . . is it possible that such monsters do in fact exist?"

Andrew stared at me. He was uncomfortable. All I wanted to do was tell him everything, was talk to him, was to be heard. This man was my beau, was the love of my life, according to Lily. I should be able to tell him these things. I wanted to open my mouth and vomit out words, everything I'd ever wanted to say but didn't. I wanted to say no to horse diving, no to playing dress-up, no to the idea of dating. Just no. I wanted to say no to everything and everyone and hear my voice ring out like church bells.

"No," said Andrew.

"Oh," I replied. I looked down at the white linen tablecloth, at the tiny empty jam jars we'd used up, the crumbs of the scones. The little delicate mess around us. I felt an urge to upend the table. Just stand up and flip it over. To create a real mess. Real chaos. To see the looks on the faces of the other people sitting so politely around us, talking in soft tones, being appropriate.

What was the point of being appropriate when life was so meaningless? When one night could change the course of your life and could destroy a living, breathing person?

A small black beetle climbed up casually onto the table-cloth and wandered across my line of vision.

"Constance," said Andrew, gently rubbing the palm of my hand with his thumb, "I have something I'd like to ask you."

"Do you see that?" I asked. I tried to pull my hand out of his, but he held fast. Just like Brant. Tight. So tight. I pulled harder. He didn't let me go. Red-hot rage started rising in my throat. "Let me go!"

I stood in a fury and Andrew rocked back slightly on his chair. I grabbed one of the empty jam jars and picked the beetle up by one of its legs, imprisoning it inside with the remaining flecks of raspberry.

"Constance, what is wrong with you?" Andrew asked, startled.

"I have to leave." I pushed my chair back and made my way toward the exit, easing myself between the tables, apologizing for getting in the way of other guests. I knew they were all staring at me. They all thought I was crazy.

I stepped out into the air and almost right into a couple going for a stroll. "I'm so sorry," I said as they looked at me, annoyed.

"Constance." Andrew grabbed me by my shoulder and I shook him off as I turned to him.

"Don't," I said.

"What's wrong? You aren't yourself. Has something happened?" He looked so concerned. He wasn't upset at all with me. He thought I was losing my mind. How could I tell him I'd never felt more like me in my life.

"Nothing has happened." I slipped the jar with the beetle in it into my pocket.

"I wanted to ask you to be my girl," he said.

I nodded. I knew he had wanted to ask something big. I had feared a proposal and felt a little relieved that he hadn't been planning one. After all, it had only been a couple weeks of courtship. The idea though that I had been dating others, that I wasn't already fully committed to him, shocked me. Did this mean he hadn't been fully committed to me the whole time?

"Have you been out on the town with other girls?" I asked. I said it lightly with a smile; I still remembered the old techniques.

"I'm a man about town," he said with a laugh. "It only reinforced how special you are." He took both my hands in his now. I couldn't. I couldn't be held by the hands. It was too visceral. I pulled them away. "Don't be upset," he said. It sounded like he was talking to a pouting puppy.

I wasn't upset with him. I was upset with myself. All this time I assumed Andrew and I were a forgone conclusion. All this time I had assumed that this was it. I had settled for him, decided the pleasantness of our interactions was good enough for me for the rest of my life. I hadn't even considered that I could still go window-shopping.

Why hadn't I considered that?

"I don't think I want to be exclusive with you," I said slowly, not being able to look him in the eyes. "I . . . need to consider myself first."

"I swear I love you, Constance. I want to marry you some-day. I promise any time spent with other girls was meaningless to me." He fidgeted awkwardly on the spot, not being able to hold me.

"How lovely for those girls," I said, almost more to myself.

"Why are you being so cruel?" he asked.

I shook my head. "I'm not. I'm not worried about what you did. I'm worried about what I didn't do."

"I don't understand." He blinked at me.

"I don't expect you to." I finally looked up at him. "Let's just leave things as they are for now. In fact, let's just leave it. Be done with all of it."

He didn't seem happy with that suggestion. But he nodded. "If that's what you want."

"It is."

It was what I wanted. It was actually exactly what I wanted. The feeling of knowing what I wanted and getting what I wanted was overpowering.

What else did I want?

"I want to go home now," I said.

"Of course," he replied.

And so I did.

"You are coming to the dinner tonight."

I had no idea why my father still insisted that I perform the dutiful son act, especially today, after everything. Did he want me to show up wrapped in bandages? Did he want me to apologize for Constance? The latter was not happening. Maybe he intended to publicly humiliate me. It was always a possibility.

I stood in front of my long mirror, looking at myself all dressed up and ready to go in my three-piece suit and pocket square. The sun had set so I had the small table lamp on beside me. It cast strange shadows and made my face look even more gaunt. I'd removed the bandages and cleaned up the cut on my forehead. It was smaller than I'd imagined under the wrappings but still stung to the touch. I pushed my hair forward to hide it. It looked unkempt, not the usual slicked-back appropriate appearance. I liked that. I liked not looking appropriate. Even as the thought twisted with discomfort in my belly.

How could I just go to a dinner after everything? How could it be night again so soon? How could I ever live through another night without thinking about everything? Without this gnawing fear in my stomach? I could hear the wind blowing outside, the branches of the large oak tree tapping at my window. This happened when the wind blew and I was used to it. As a child I'd been so scared of it, thinking a ghost was floating just outside, and I'd hide my head under the covers for fear of seeing anything. The branches tapped again and I was compelled for some reason this time to glance over at the window, at the darkness that loomed just outside the house.

A black silhouette of a face.

Outside my second-story window.

I stumbled backward, tripping on my heels, my heart beating fast. It was impossible. It was a trick of the light surely. Old memories haunting me.

I looked again.

The face was gone.

I steadied myself and took in a deep breath. I was terrified but I approached the window slowly to see, to look out. I looked out at the tree branches creaking in the wind. I saw the road and the sidewalk. I saw emptiness.

I knew what was happening. I had read enough books to know how people dealing with guilt and fear manifested their nightmares as reality. It was all my fault. All of it. I had been told to keep it a secret, and what had I done? Shown it off like some trophy because I liked a girl.

So it was Constance's fault then.

No. No, that was wrong and thoughtless. Something my

father would say. He would find anyone else to blame, he was a master at it.

I backed away slowly from the window and turned into my room. I noticed then just how dark it was. How the single lamp by the mirror made the corners all that much darker. Like shadows seeping into the room.

I tried to shake the feeling and returned to the mirror to straighten my tie. My hands were trembling, but I was almost used to that now. Fear was just starting to become a part of me. Never leaving, always there, in charge.

I heard a sound. And whipped around to look into the dark corner of my room. There was nothing. Of course there was nothing.

Why couldn't I control this fear? It was unmanly and unmannerly. Have some self-control, Bill. You aren't a child anymore. You're almost eighteen. There aren't ghosts outside your window. There aren't monsters under the bed or hiding in the shadows.

And yet . . .

They do exist underground. Here. In Atlantic City. Not so far away.

My eyes focused in on the dark. On the empty nothingness. I felt that pull like I had in the room with the machine. I felt drawn into the darkness. It reminded me of that feeling when you are standing on a high balcony and looking down at the ground. You know you aren't going to jump . . . but maybe . . .

I shook my head. No. No, I refused to allow my mind to go there.

I turned back to the mirror and saw a tall black silhouette standing behind me.

I jumped and turned. My heart in my throat. My breath constricted and tight.

Nothing. No one.

But still in my mind's eye I could see the figure. Faceless, like a shadow. I stared into the darkness once more. I took in a deep breath and walked slowly toward the corner, reaching my hands out in front of me, just to see, just to know, just to touch. I must be losing my mind.

My fingers touched the wall. I found only empty blackness and the spot where two walls met. I released a sigh and felt my body relax even if my mind was still racing. I turned and leaned against the wall, staring now at the lamp that seemed far away somehow even if it was just across the room. This was a kind of madness. It had to be. I slid down and sat on the ground. I placed my hands next to me on the floor just to ground me. To make me solid and not a mass of shaking jelly.

The floor was wet.

I raised my hands.

They were covered in black ink.

"There's my boy, better late than never," boomed my father as I entered the private room on the second floor of the restaurant. I felt strangely winded from the climb, but I knew it wasn't because of the stairs. I had rushed to change my inky clothes and then hide them under the bed like a child hiding an inappropriate novel from a parent. My hands were still stained no matter how hard I washed them. Fainter now, but still with a coating of black. I had put on gloves but already I was feeling too warm.

I was a disaster. I couldn't do this. But I had to. So I smiled and laughed and gave an awkward wave at the gathered crowd. It was more than just the men from New York this time, I was relieved to see. There was also the usual gang I was familiar seeing at my father's parties. There was Mr. Brown. And Madame Turcotte and her daughter. And Mr. and Mrs. Sawyer being quietly shy on the edges of the crowd. There were also a few others I didn't recognize. Everyone was milling about, drinking cocktails, and I joined Madame Turcotte and said hello.

"My goodness but you are growing up fast," she said as we kissed the air beside each other's cheeks.

"Well, you don't change a bit," I replied. She laughed and I felt myself relax slightly. Mindless small talk, there was a comfort in that.

". . . Gent. It's a contracting firm based here with offices all over the Eastern Seaboard."

I turned so fast, my drink sloshed over the side of my glass. I stared at one of the most beautiful women I'd ever seen. And I had seen plenty here in Atlantic City. We didn't just have singers and dancers; we had guests from all over the world and we hosted the Miss America Pageant. And yet I stared at this woman. She seemed to glow from the inside out, dressed in an all-white satin gown that glinted in the light. Her hair was so blonde that it almost matched. She was an angel.

The angel noticed me.

"Yes?" she asked with her lovely melodic voice.

"I'm so sorry, I heard you say something about Gent?" I floated over to her. It felt suddenly as if there was no one else in the room.

She smiled and I just about died—it felt like an arrow to the heart, but in a strangely good way.

"My boyfriend is a manager for the company," she said.

"Your boyfriend."

I thought of Mr. Connor. Gruff, rough-around-the-edges Mr. Connor. Was he the manager? I thought he was, but he couldn't be, could he? Not if this elegant creature was the manager's partner.

"Yes."

"Thomas Connor, fine fellow, brilliant mind, tedious conversationalist." A tall man in an elegant suit and a twinkle in his eye joined us. "Joey Drew," he said, extending his hand. I took it. Wasn't he the man Mr. Connor had been talking about? My memory was foggy, filled only with images from last night. I couldn't push past them all to focus on the conversation.

"It's nice to meet you," I said as we shook hands. "I'm Bill Chambers."

"The son!" said Joey.

"I am."

"Well, it's a pleasure. This lovely creature is the famous actress Allison Pendle. I assume you've heard of her." I smiled to indicate I had, but to be perfectly honest, I had not. "If you haven't heard of her, you've definitely heard her. She voices my darling Alice Angel."

Alice Angel? Why was that so familiar?

Joey Drew . . .

"You're the animation man," I said, finally understanding. "Joey Drew Studios. The Bendy cartoons!"

Joey smiled at me, slightly tight-lipped. I didn't think I'd said anything wrong. It had taken me a moment with the state of my brain to remember, but I had in the end.

"I love your cartoons," I said. It wasn't quite true. I'd seen them as a child, and I believe there had been some war bond advertisements with the characters as well. I had little memory of them. "Boris is my favorite," I added.

"Well, thank you," replied Joey, still tight-lipped.

Quickly change the subject, I thought. This was going quite badly for some reason. "And what brings the two of you to Atlantic City?"

"Well, son, I've always been a fan. I love places that light up the world. This city is like a living, breathing amusement park. You familiar with Bertrum Piedmont?" asked Joey with a renewed energy.

I shook my head no.

"He's an incredible park engineer. He's working on some

new projects for me and he suggested I make a visit to see the new developments happening here. Said I should ring your dad!"

"If there's something being built, my father is financing it," I said.

"Your father does well for himself," said Joey. It was a statement that felt like a question.

"I suppose he does, yes."

Joey smiled. "Well, maybe someday he and I will work together on something. I do like working with the best."

That was my in. "And you also work with Thomas Connor, correct?"

Joey's smile faltered slightly. "I do."

"I heard there were some complications over some machine or other?" Careful, Bill, my gut told me. This was dangerous territory. I couldn't let them know what had happened, that I knew there were dark secrets about that machine. But I needed to know more. If not for my own sake, for Constance's. Brave Constance, who told my father what was what and did it with her chin held high.

"Who told you that?" asked Joey.

"Mr. Connor himself."

"You know my Tom?" asked Allison sweetly. There was no hint of digging at something deeper in how she spoke.

"Yes, I do," I replied. I turned to her and was immediately overcome by her radiance once more. "I work with Gent some-times. As a lark. I enjoy fixing things. I've met Mr. Connor on occasion."

"This machine you mention, have you seen it?" asked Joey. That fear, that feeling that had haunted me ever since yesterday, filled me top full just then. He couldn't know that I had seen it. He couldn't know any of the things I knew. I wouldn't tell him.

"No, I don't really know what it is. He didn't talk much about it, just that it had been a project for someone in New York."

"He said that, did he?" The man looked very different suddenly, like a dark cloud had passed over him. Nothing had changed, not his smile or his posture, but I could sense something dangerous.

"What does it do?" I asked. I hadn't meant to be so direct. I had intended to be quite the opposite. To stop talking about the subject. To compliment Allison's dress. To walk away and stand in a corner until dinner was served. But somehow I asked my most desired question. The question I'd had since that day Mr. Connor and I fixed the machine: *What does it do?*

Allison laughed then, a laugh that danced happily in the air. "You will never get these boys to tell you anything about their secret inventions. Trust me, I've tried." She winked at me.

Joey leaned in, and with a slight smile he said, "Have you ever considered, my boy, that your reality is no more real than a dream I had last night?"

"I . . . had not considered that, no," I replied.

"Well, consider it now."

"I . . . will."

The little dinner bell was rung at just that moment. A

little saving grace in a strange situation. I parted ways with them and took my assigned seat down the table between Mrs. Sawyer and Mr. Brown. Two very harmless people who loved my father unconditionally and therefore I could say nothing accidentally to ruin his reputation. For my part, I was glad to be far away from the animator and the voice actress.

I had no idea what he meant, and I had no desire to consider my own existence in that way. I did think for a moment that my reality was so unbelievable that it could only be a nightmare for him. Maybe he was right in that way.

Maybe everyone was right.

Maybe Constance had a point. These people—Mr. Connor, Joey, even the magnificent Allison—these people were different somehow. They were up to something unnatural. What we had experienced, what had happened to Brant, that was not something that just happened. That was something created by humans. Like the bombs that fell from the sky during the war.

What sort of people invented something like that? What sort of people held a creature that stalked its prey like that, underground, down in the secret places that still exist from secret pasts?

I needed to speak with Constance again. I needed to tell her about these people.

I needed to tell her she was right.

32: CONSTANCE

I held the little jar delicately in my hand. The beetle crawled along the inside, trying to find an escape but falling onto its back instead. There was something about staring at this little living creature that made me hesitate. Then I wondered why. What was I afraid of? I had planned on squishing it when I first spotted it in the restaurant, stomping on it and walking away with no further thought.

Still.

I shivered.

The walls of our apartment were thin, silly and useless. Silly and useless. I turned the jar around and the beetle fell again, its little legs flailing.

I stared at it. Then I imagined being the beetle in the bottle. Imagined being watched closely and carefully. Examined.

I suddenly looked over my shoulder. It felt like maybe Molly or Lily was standing quietly in the doorway but no one was there. Just the dark hallway. I felt very aware now of myself, of being in the small pool of light at my desk. How vulnerable that could appear. How vulnerable I felt.

I felt aware too of the darkness as an alive thing. Like the creeping shadows that had stalked us the other night. I had a vision of the blackness outside my door suddenly bursting in a wave into my room, swallowing me up, drowning me.

Standing quickly, I marched over to the door and shut it. I felt a wave of relief. Then that familiar feeling of anger. I was frustrated with myself for being so weak, for fearing monsters in the dark. Whatever we had encountered was far away and locked underground.

Or was it?

Well, I was determined to find out, with or without the help of stupid knucklehead boys. The problem was getting back to the machine.

I heard a strange sob then. Quiet and almost like the wind or the creaking of floorboards. But it wasn't. It wasn't my imagination either. It was a soft desperate sound. Someone was in pain. Was it one of my sisters? I stood and clambered over my bed to the wall and placed my ear against it. Silence. Good, Molly and Lily were well.

I got up and went to the opposite wall I shared with my parents and did the same. More silence. I turned and listened carefully, straining to hear the sound again. I closed my eyes, as if shutting off the other senses might help make this one stronger.

Something grabbed me hard by the wrist.

I opened my eyes and yanked my arm away. "Get off me!" I shouted to the empty dark corner in front of me.

I whirled around. Nothing. Nobody. I marched toward the switch for the overhead light and turned it on. My room filled with light and I examined it carefully. Again there was nothing. No. This wasn't right. I didn't believe it was my imagination. Someone was playing a game with me. I glanced at the light switch that I still held between my fingers and noticed then the black stain at my wrist on the sleeve of my nightgown. A black handprint where I had been grabbed. Wet and fresh and oh so there.

I wasn't frightened then. I felt anger that something had dared to attack me. I felt anger that it had just run away, disappeared like a coward. You want to fight me, attack me, drag me away, and kill me? Just you try it. I was feeling so energized, my skin was buzzing. I could face anything right now. This anger was fuel; it was amazing.

I raced back to my desk and opened the little jar. The beetle couldn't quite climb out of it and that was good because I needed my other hand for this. I grabbed at the sleeve of my nightgown and squeezed the fresh black ooze into the jar, like wringing out a towel after washing the dishes. Several drops fell into the jar and onto the beetle. I smiled and quickly sealed the jar up again.

I looked at my hand as it stained black prints on the outside of the jar.

And I smiled.

Now we would wait and see.

33: BILL

I stared at the black stain on

my floor the next morning. In the light of day I had hoped for some logical explanation. Like how a shadowy figure in the night turns out to be a coat rack by day. But no, my floor was stained with black ink. It had dried, but before it had, it had wandered. I could see the jagged reaching stain, those fingers of ink. Just like in the Prohibition factory, just like over Brant's body, the ink had clawed itself forward, searching for something. It had not found it.

There had been a monster in my room last night. Was it the same one that had clawed at my ankle in the dark? I assumed so. How could it not be? The thought that there was more than one was too much for me to handle. I quickly dragged my armchair into the corner, hiding the ink beneath it. I didn't need any of the servants trying to clean it up and getting in trouble.

I dressed quickly and with great purpose and left my house only to stop a few blocks away and realize I had no idea where I was going. How was I to find Constance? Finding me was much easier; our house was well known, the largest in the neighborhood. But to find someone who helped dress chorus girls and lived with her sisters and parents in a city like this? That was a much harder task.

The chorus girls.

That was it! I could meet her at the theater tonight. That would do the trick. I would apologize and tell her what happened last night, all of it, the ink, meeting that Joey Drew fellow.

Of course there was now an afternoon to fill until then.

I had another idea.

●●●●●●●●●●●●●●●●●●●●●●●

I was brought a coffee as I sat on the plush green settee in the foyer of the hotel. "Thank you, Johnson," I said. The old man in the Plaza uniform nodded and turned and I had a memory then of playing hide-and-seek with him when I was young. The hotel had been my playground, and I had loved it even more than the beach just outside.

Now the hotel just felt like a weight pressing down on me, a reminder of things to come. There were days I wanted to run away from it all. Start a new life, maybe on the West Coast. Things there seemed bright and fresh. Everyone had left something behind. When I turned eighteen maybe I would.

Maybe.

The problem with fear is that while running can feel just

perfect, there is also a fear of actually running away. Of what that would mean, of where to go and who to be. Of being without the safety net of my father's connections and wealth.

Why was I so afraid? It was exhausting but the feeling just persisted, on and on, lingering, like a toothache.

He entered the lobby like he was walking onto a stage. There he was, in his finely tailored pinstripe suit, the Mister Joey Drew from last night. I sank deep into the settee and pulled my hat low. I could see his feet now as he almost danced his way across the floor. His shoes were freshly polished and made of a fine leather. I'd not seen shoes that well made in a long time. I wondered at the man's wealth. He was too showy for it to be old money, that was for certain.

He was joined then by another pair of shoes, or, should I say, boots. Those I recognized, though I did find it interesting I'd noticed them at all in the first place. They were brown and well worn and huge. I was surprised to see them. My plan had been just to keep an eye on this Joey person, but there he was. This made things a little more difficult. I sank lower.

"Tom, my good man, it's wonderful to see you again," said the shiny shoes.

"Let's go," replied the boots.

"Always in a hurry," replied the shiny shoes.

"Just like getting the job done." The boots turned and made their way toward the exit. The shiny shoes stayed still for a moment and then followed.

I raised my hat and watched the retreating backs of Mr.

Connor and Joey. I had to follow them. I had to do it quickly. Even as my nerves kept me rooted to the spot.

I managed to jump to my feet, spilling some coffee on the green settee. I looked down. The dark liquid seeped into the fabric and disappeared. I clenched my fists. I was still wearing gloves; the ink on my hands was almost gone but not quite.

Not quite.

I had to follow them. I chased after them out of the hotel and ran right into Mr. Connor. I fell backward, onto the side-walk, right onto my backside. It was like running face-first into a wall.

"You following us, Bill?" asked Mr. Connor, looking down at me. Joey joined him and together they loomed over me like distorted cartoon characters. Which was fitting, I supposed.

"No, Mr. Connor," I replied.

"Come on, could use your help." Mr. Connor extended a meaty hand and I took it. He helped me up to standing.

"Are you sure this is a good idea?" asked Joey, who seemed quite sure of the answer.

"Could use the help. He's helped before." Mr. Connor turned and started walking again as Joey and I stared at each other.

"If you knew about the machine, why didn't you say so?" asked Joey.

I wasn't sure if he was trying to trick me, but at this point honesty felt like the best policy. "I was keeping a secret for Mr. Connor."

Joey thought about that and then suddenly his whole disposition brightened. "Well, that is something, isn't it?" He smiled and gave me a hearty pat on the back. "We'd better catch up. Don't want to get on Tom's bad side," he said with a grin.

I smiled back, not sure if I was considered a friend yet, but I was happy to have won him over for the moment. We walked speedily to catch up with Mr. Connor, who was waiting for us by his truck. As I climbed in and got squished in the middle of the bench, I asked, "What about Scott?"

Mr. Connor didn't say anything. He just started the truck and we were on our way.

Considering the company and the direction we were heading, I assumed our end destination would be the Prohibition factory. I was not happy about this, but what had I expected to find if I had followed them? Of course this is where they were going and I simply had to deal with the very real fact that I was about to enter a place where I had seen a man explode and where a monster had chased me in the dark.

I laughed to myself at the everyday thought of "simply having to deal" with it. This was not really something one simply did.

"What amuses you, friend?" asked Joey.

"Oh, it's nothing," I replied absentmindedly, rubbing my hands together.

He didn't press, which was good because for the life of me I couldn't think of a single joke I could use as my excuse.

Knock knock!

Who's there?

Brant.

Brant who?

That was all my mind could tell me, repeating the same phrase over and over. Brant who, indeed. Did he have family? Were they missing him? Would the police start looking for him?

Brant who?

We pulled to a stop, and as usual and with no ceremony, Mr. Connor opened his door and jumped out of the truck. I was shocked. We weren't at the factory. We were in a grimy little part of town at a dirty little corner bar evidently called The Way Out.

Joey opened his door casually and slipped out of the truck even as Mr. Connor walked with purpose and opened the door to the bar. He had disappeared inside before Joey could accidentally close the truck door in my face.

"Sorry about that, kid," he said with a grin, and opened it again.

I smiled and stepped onto the sidewalk, staring at the bar. I didn't understand anything right now but I wished Constance was with me.

We stepped into the dark dingy bar, both of us removing our hats as we did so and looking around. It was early afternoon so there weren't many people there, and those who were seemed like they always had been, as if they were part of the furniture. Dust particles floated in the sunbeams and landed on drink rings on tables but seemed to illuminate nothing else.

"Come on," said Mr. Connor from across the room. He was at a door by the sticky bar and we followed him into a back room of dark-paneled wood. There was a table and chairs piled up on top of it. There was stale smell in the air, and when I walked over to join Mr. Connor by one of the wood panels, my shoes stuck to the floor slightly with each step.

"This is not exactly what I had in mind, Tom," said Joey, sticky-stepping his way to us.

"I told you the other entrance is out of order," replied Mr. Connor.

Other entrance.

"You fix things for a living, Tom," replied Joey.

Mr. Connor shook his head and pressed on the wood panel. It slipped back an inch from the wall and he dragged it then to the side. "Some things are just broken for good." He stepped through the hole.

I didn't think it good form to follow, so I extended my hand to allow Joey the right of way. He took it without even acknowledging me and I followed behind him into the dark.

We found ourselves in a tunnel sloping downward on a steady decline. It flattened out soon enough and Mr. Connor turned on a flashlight ahead of us. "Stay to the right," he ordered, and just as he did, my leg caught the edge of something and I stumbled forward.

"Ow."

Mr. Connor turned the flashlight on me and then to the left of the tunnel as if pointing with it. There was a metal table next to us. Or no. Not a table. As Mr. Connor dragged the light along the wall, it revealed a long conveyor belt.

"For crates, kid," said Joey, beside me. "Crates of liquor."

I nodded.

"Okay, enough sightseeing," said Mr. Connor. He aimed the flashlight in front of him, lighting the large tunnel and showcasing the black void in the distance. His hulking silhouette led the way and we followed him, a point of light with darkness behind us and darkness before us.

I understood now what was happening, and dread filled me with every step we took. Obviously there would be more than one entrance into the whiskey factory. That there was another way out that entire time. That we could have gone out a different way, that Brant . . .

Brant who?

Something darted across the path of light in front of us.

"Did you see that?" I asked, stopping short.

But no one else stopped. They just kept walking, the light getting farther away from me, the darkness surrounding me. Like shadows climbing up a wall. I ran to catch up and held my breath as we approached the spot where I'd seen the something.

Nothing happened.

So I let out my breath in a long silent sigh.

"Bill!"

I cried out as I fell flat on my face onto the rough floor, something heavy on my back. Something that knew my name. I tried to push it off, tried to turn over, but it was squirming and fighting back, leaning hard on me so my face was rubbing roughly against the gravel on the ground. I couldn't even cry for help—the wind was being crushed out of me. I heard the sounds of a scuffle above me then. I heard the sounds of a fight. Yells and then a mighty grunt as the something was pulled off me in one swoop.

I scrambled onto my back, sitting there on the cold cement floor, panting hard, trying desperately to fill up my lungs as fast as I could. The flashlight had fallen and was shining directly at Joey's gleaming shoes. In the distance I could see the faint shadow of Mr. Connor in a struggle. I quickly reached over to grab the flashlight as I got to my feet. I shone it at Mr. Connor, over Joey's shoulder.

Mr. Connor was holding a figure upright, a hand at each side of his upper torso. He wasn't just holding him upright, he was holding him dangling in the air, his toes just grazing the ground. The figure's clothes and hair were drenched in black ink, but he was not covered completely, not like Brant had been. This figure, you could see his face, his wild eyes.

It was Scott.

"What's going on?!" I demanded.

"Cool down," said Mr. Connor to Scott as he thrashed about in the air.

"He's coming; he's coming for you all!" he screamed. He suddenly looked directly at me, at the beam of light. His eyes glowed in the light and his face contorted into a grotesque grimace.

"Make him quiet," said Joey, coming up beside me in an angry hiss.

"How do you think I should do that?" asked Mr. Connor, glancing at us. His arms were straining with the effort of holding the twisting Scott.

"Just do it," ordered Joey.

"It's all your fault," Scott spat at Joey. "You're the real monster!"

"Tom!"

"How are you going to silence me, Drew? What do you want him to do to me?" Scott started laughing. It was high-pitched and pierced my ears. The sound echoed in the tunnel.

"Do it!" ordered Joey.

Scott thrashed around again and Mr. Connor struggled to keep hold of him. He twisted and turned and then leaned down and bit Mr. Connor's hand. Instinctively Mr. Connor let go and Scott wrenched himself out of his grip and immediately ran off into the dark. There was a hollow thud in the blackness as Mr. Connor and I raced to follow him.

Scott was lying on the ground, unconscious. The tunnel had turned at a ninety-degree angle and he had charged right into it. I reached up and touched the wound on my forehead. I thought about how I got it.

I backed away slowly from Scott.

"Good," said Joey, joining us. "Leave him here to sleep it off. Come on." He grabbed the flashlight out of my hand and continued down the tunnel.

Mr. Connor carefully adjusted Scott to make him more comfortable and then stared at his body for a quiet moment. The light got dimmer and dimmer, and as I stared at Scott and Mr. Connor, I felt the need to say something.

"What did he mean by 'monster'?" I asked quietly.

"I already told you about that," he replied.

"What is going on? Please tell me." I sounded pathetic. I sounded too desperate, like a small child. My father would not have approved. I was not coming at this conversation from a place of "authority."

"I can't," said Mr. Connor quietly. He stood up and looked at the light disappearing down the tunnel in the distance. "We need to fix the machine, and then take it back to New York ASAP."

"Okay," I said, but inside I was a mess of anxiety and fear. How could they possibly do that? How could they move the machine at all knowing there was some creature on the loose? Would they just leave it here to haunt Atlantic City for all time? Or . . . or would they take it to one of the biggest cities in America? To potentially unleash all the horrors there?

"Let's go," said Mr. Connor.

"I can't." I couldn't. I couldn't go back there, I couldn't. I couldn't be a part of this. Not after everything I'd seen.

"Don't be a fool, come on." I could barely see Mr. Connor anymore. Joey had left us literally in the dark.

"No." Who did he think he was, ordering me around? I was William Chambers, the heir to all of Atlantic City. Heck,

I probably owned these tunnels as well. I turned on my heel and started retracing my steps in the dark.

"Bill!" called out Mr. Connor, but I was done. I was not going to end up like Brant or Scott. I knew deep down how close I'd come. How close I *was*. I felt a madness inside me that I had assumed was a human reaction to a horrific situation, but now, now I wasn't sure. Now I didn't know what was happening to me.

I turned the corner and picked up speed. It was a straight shot to the bar now. When the ground started to rise, I felt a wave of relief and I burst into the back room from behind the panel like water breaking through a dam.

I stood in the room for a moment and collected myself as best I could, though the fear would not go away.

I thought long and hard.

I needed to find Constance.

34: CONSTANCE

The beetle was dead.

Not because of the ink; it hadn't been poisoned. I'd watched it all night as it got more and more agitated. As it raced in tiny circles in the jar. As it wore itself out and then just stopped moving. I'd opened the jar then and carefully taken it out, laying it on a cloth on my desk.

The ink had had an effect on its behavior, that much I understood. But what kind of effect, I didn't fully understand. Had it made the beetle want to run and run? It seemed a very specific kind of reaction that was too particular.

I tried to stay calm in my frustration. I wanted answers. I needed answers. But when Molly knocked on my door, I was too quick to yell at her, too angry at her for interrupting me. What did she think she was doing? I was trying to solve a delicate problem.

What was the ink?

"Mother wants help with breakfast," she said, sounding surprised at my response.

"I'm sick," I said bluntly.

"Oh no, did you catch my cold?" She sounded genuinely concerned. Of course she did. She was the sweetest, kindest girl. I always tried to be just like her. But I wasn't her. I had complicated and messy thoughts I wanted to shout from the rooftops. I hated to think it, but in so many ways I was more like Lily, except Lily had no reservations just being herself.

What was I? Who was I?

I shook my head to knock the thought out of it. Then I looked at my sleeve. The inky black handprint. I wasn't scared. I was determined.

"Yes," I said.

"Oh dear. Would you like me to bring you some soup? Some tea?"

"Just go away." I didn't shout, but there was an edge in my voice. I was so close to the solution and she kept interrupting me. I had this vision then of sitting on the Ferris wheel at the Steel Pier, sitting at the very top.

And just screaming.

I sighed hard. I felt a wave of exhaustion pass over me. I had, after all, been up all night. But it was more than that. It was something deep inside me. Something buried deep, a part of my soul that had been crying out for so long and was so very tired.

I stared at the beetle.

It had run and run and run until it was so very tired.

Something clicked inside me. Could it be? Oh how I wished

I could talk to Bill about all this. I wished he cared. How could he not care? It was so unfeeling, so dismissive and horrible. Rich boys and their lack of empathy.

I stood in a rush of anger and let out a frustrated yell. My chair fell backward and onto the floor.

"Are you alright?" It was Molly again at the door.

"Yes, I'm perfectly fine," I said, balling my hands into fists. But I wasn't. This wasn't normal. Even though it felt right, even though I'd never felt more like myself, none of this was normal. Sharing my feelings, letting them take over, not being in control.

It all clicked together.

The ink. The ink was doing something to me. Even though I had washed it all away, I clearly hadn't. Somewhere inside me it lurked, and it was unleashing these tightly kept feelings, these carefully concealed emotions. I didn't want to run in circles, but I did want to be free.

I picked up my chair and sat again at my desk.

My gloves were still sitting there in the middle of all my little vials and experiments. I took in a deep breath. It was time to clean them.

35. BILL

I stood outside the door to the backstage like some ridiculous fan as the waiters prepared the tables for dinner service. I felt absurd just standing here. Waiting, knowing that down in the deep depths men were working on a machine that would destroy us all. Next to me was a fellow holding a bouquet of flowers, waiting for his girl to show up for work, no doubt. He looked so normal, so very unaware of the evil happening right now.

Where was she? Why wasn't she here yet? A dozen girls had already passed us by and giggled at the man holding the flowers, yet no Constance to be seen.

I shifted in place. My nerves were so frayed, it felt like I was going to jump out of my own skin.

"Andrew!" A familiar-looking girl with dark black hair done up perfectly in victory rolls, in a simple but charming red coat, bounded over to the man with the flowers. I expected some sort of embrace, but instead she stopped short and just smiled at him. "What are you doing here?"

The man smiled. "Hello, Lily. I'm waiting for your sister," he replied.

"Oh, she's not feeling well today. Shall I take the flowers for her?" She reached out expectantly.

"She's not?" he asked, looking quite thoughtful.

"Just a cold. You needn't worry like this." Lily was looking a little annoyed.

"I need to see her."

"There isn't anything I can do about that. Now give me the flowers. I promise I'll take them to her." At this point the girl reached out to grab the flowers but Andrew yanked them back.

"No, I'm going to her."

Lily sighed hard. "Fine then. She's at home; you can find her there. Tell her I tried to be a good sister. She won't believe you." She grinned. "Bill, are you waiting for her too?"

Suddenly the girl was looking right at me and that's when I remembered her from the Boardwalk. Of course! She was Constance's sister. Wait, was that the sister they had been talking about just now?

"I am. You say she's at home, she's not well?"

Lily nodded and made to speak but she was interrupted gruffly by Andrew. "Why are you looking for Constance?" he asked.

Andrew and I stared at each other. There was something going on inside him, something that seemed more than just a potentially jealous beau. Then again, there was always something else going on inside us, something secret we never tell anyone else. A deep terrible fear of the future maybe? Or was that just me?

"We're friends," I said.

"Andrew, this is William Chambers," said Lily in a meaningful tone. "You know who Mr. Chambers is, don't you?"

Andrew nodded but still looked at me closely.

"Shall we go together to see her?" I asked, trying to sound friendly. I also thought this was a perfect solution to my problem, considering I had no idea where she lived.

Andrew nodded again. The man had gone mute.

"Come, I'll pay for the jitney," I said.

Andrew scoffed at that. "I'm surprised someone like you doesn't own a fancy car."

"I do, I just hate driving," I replied. I hated everything about it, the speed, the danger. To be in control of something that could easily spin out of control. I shivered at the thought.

"Fine, let's go." Andrew walked off suddenly toward the exit, holding the flowers down and letting them just swing in his hand as if they weren't delicate things easily destroyed.

Then again, I realized as I followed him, technically they were already dead.

CONSTANCE

There was a time when my sister

telling me that two boys were waiting outside to see me would have filled me with joy. I had always dreamed of being able to attract the attention of multiple suitors. In this moment, however, it was the last thing I was interested in. I had organized a series of test tubes and was working on a literal solution to eliminate the ink. I had discovered that adding some iron oxide into the mix was having an amazing result. I didn't have time for boys who were annoyed with me. And what's more, I was the one more annoyed with them.

It made me question my old desire for suitors in the first place. Was romance something I was interested in or was pleasing my parents and getting married and helping support the family more the goal? Was anything in my life really about what I wanted?

I huffed and stood up, feeling so frustrated. I didn't care to see either of them, and I didn't care to waste any more time than needed, so I slipped on my winter boots and grabbed my lined blue dressing gown.

I rushed past Molly, still standing by my door, and through the kitchen before anyone could comment. I did hear Mother say, "You can't go out like that!" But what did it matter? What did anything matter? I didn't care what anyone thought.

I stormed downstairs and glared at Mrs. Wilson as she peeked around her ground-floor door, the chain still on. I flung open the front door to the building. Standing there before me was Andrew, seething with a bouquet of flowers, and Bill, looking like he'd seen a ghost.

"What?" I asked, putting my hands on my hips.

"You act so demure and so hurt, and yet you are a hypocrite, Miss Gray," said Andrew, tossing the flowers onto the ground.

"I beg your pardon?" I asked. I wanted to laugh. These poor little flowers on my stoop. They hadn't done anything wrong. For that matter, neither had I.

"You're dating William Chambers," he said, pointing to Bill standing right next to him.

"Now see here," said Bill, all flustered.

"Oh, please," I replied with a very hearty roll of the eyes. This was absurd. "Your jealousy is making you irrational."

"Then what is he doing looking for you at the theater?"

"He's my friend, Andrew. You do know about friends, don't you?"

"Sarcasm does not become you," he said.

"Well, pouting doesn't become you!" I shook my head and looked at them both. I stood at the top of the three small steps;

231

it gave me enough height that I felt literally above them both. Though, to be honest, I was rather glad to see Bill. I had so much to say to him.

"What happened to the sweet, shy girl I wanted to go steady with?" Andrew asked, shaking his head.

"That's the problem, Andrew. I was never sweet or shy. You were just too busy talking about yourself to notice. And maybe that was my fault, maybe I should have spoken up sooner. I don't know. I don't know why I was always so quiet anymore, really."

"Well, why can't you be like that again?"

Now I laughed. I closed my eyes and shook my head and I found that laughing this way felt freeing, like yelling or throwing something. It wasn't quite the same, but I felt this pressure release like a kettle whistling.

"Don't laugh at me."

I opened my eyes. "Don't ask me such a stupid question again then!"

"Enough of this, the both of you," said Bill in that way he sometimes spoke, imitating his father. I wondered if he knew how silly he looked. Like a small child wearing their parent's shoes.

"You should leave now, Andrew," I said. I stared him down. He for his part attempted to do likewise, and I wondered if all those staring contests with my sisters had actually had a practical purpose in the end.

"The lady has asked you to leave," said Bill, interrupting the battle.

Andrew looked at Bill and then back again. "If I leave now, then that's it; it's over between us."

"Andrew, it was over between us when I left you at the teahouse. You don't get to take that away from me to make yourself feel better." I had no idea where the words were coming from and how they flowed so easily, but it felt incredible.

No, I did know where they came from. I just didn't care right at this moment. In this moment I was happy to let the feelings have free rein.

"You're just like your sisters—you don't care about romance, you just want attention from men," he said, leaning in.

And then he was leaning away, holding his face with his hands. I hadn't known I had the ability to slap a person. I'd never done such a thing before, but it had felt easy and right.

"Don't you ever say anything about my sisters. Don't you ever come near any of my family again!" I was ready to launch myself at him. I wanted to hit him again. How dare he!

"Constance, no!" said Bill, putting himself between us. "Andrew, you need to leave."

"I'm gone. She's bonkers." He staggered away. I fumed, watching him retreat like a dog with his tail between his legs.

"You should have let me at him, Bill," I said.

"No, I don't think I should have. Though he would have deserved it. Are you okay?" he asked.

"I've never felt better," I replied. I finally shifted my focus to him. "What are you doing here anyway?"

Bill still looked concerned and it was starting to annoy me.

233

He was here for a reason and yet somehow Andrew had ruined that as well.

"Bill," I said. "Please. What are you doing here?"

He nodded and said, "I've learned so much about the machine in the last day, I have to tell you everything."

I stared at him. I had anticipated an apology or possibly that he wanted to ask me out on a date himself. But that he had been doing the very thing he had told me not to, I was both upset and impressed.

"Did you lie to me then, to protect me in some grand gesture?" I asked.

"No, absolutely not." He stopped and thought about that. "Not that I wouldn't want to protect you, but I swear that I thought it was the best course of action at the time. I still do."

"You still do?" Now I was confused. I smiled at Mr. Sweet and his little boy as they walked by and waved. "I think we need to go inside. We don't have the benefit of space like in your neighborhood. We're being watched." It sounded ominous, but it wasn't. It was just a fact that Mrs. Fielding across the street on the second floor was absolutely watching us through her lace curtains. The street enjoyed a good gossip.

"Okay," said Bill, looking a little worried. I opened the door and he took off his hat passing over the threshold.

We walked in silence up the stairs and, as we approached my apartment, I took in a quiet breath. Bringing home a boy was not something any of us girls did. For Lily it was because she never took any of her beaux seriously enough to bring home; for

Molly it was because she preferred her privacy. And for me, well, for me it was because I never, before Andrew, had had a boy to bring home in the first place. Bill would be welcomed with open arms and that was part of the problem. The son of Mr. Chambers in our apartment. I worried my mother would be embarrassed without the notice to clean everything and my father would be aware of his poverty. I worried what Bill would think, if he would think less of me. He always seemed to think I walked on water, or at the least I was impressive for diving into it.

All of this I thought in a moment but I didn't pause before opening the door and loudly announcing, "Bill Chambers has come to visit!"

My mother and Molly came over, all smiles. They were already dressed to go take in Lily's new show, my mother hat in hand and Molly wrapping her scarf around her neck. They froze on the spot as he entered the apartment.

Father meanwhile stood casually from his armchair, folding the paper and placing it in his seat. He looked very much as if he'd been expecting Bill and was not remotely taken aback by his presence. He and Bill shook hands.

"Lad, you just missed dinner. Can I offer you a coffee?" he asked.

"I'm fine, Mr. Gray," replied Bill, all politeness.

"Constance, dear, why don't you change into something more appropriate," my mother said, hiding her mortification that I was in my dressing gown in such company, but I knew she was feeling it acutely.

"I'm fine," I replied. "I'm going to show Bill my chemistry set." I motioned for Bill to follow me.

"I'm not so sure about that, young lady," said my mother. My father reached for his coat and nodded in agreement.

I didn't have time for their sudden old-fashioned behavior. "He is coming with me to my room, and you will trust me," I said curtly.

My mother looked at me with some surprise. I was getting used to this now.

"Constance," said Molly, as a way of gently telling me what I said was unkind.

"Please, I'm under the weather, just let me do this," I said. "You all go to the theater. I promise everything will be just fine."

My mother and father looked at each other, and finally Mother nodded slowly. What could they do really? They could say no, but how often did any of their girls bring back a boy of such high standing as a Chambers? The three of them left, with Molly mouthing "Be good" to me as they did. I hated that Mother didn't approve but I also knew that there were more important things happening right now than what she thought. So I quickly led Bill down the narrow hall and into my bedroom, closing the door behind us. Only then did I feel the weight of social propriety fall heavy on my shoulders. I was alone in my bedroom with a boy. My cheeks got red and I hoped Bill didn't notice.

"This is incredible," he said. He had made a beeline for my

desk, not seeming to have the same concerns. Once again I felt anger at the double standard; it didn't even occur to him that a reputation could be injured this way. Why would it? He was protected by virtue of being a boy, and a rich boy at that.

I quickly joined him. "I've learned so much about the ink," I said.

"And I've learned so much about the machine."

"Tell me everything."

Bill looked up at me and then glanced around the room as if someone might be lurking in the evening shadows that were growing up my walls. Maybe there was. I glanced toward the corner where I had been grabbed and instinctively pulled the wrist of my dressing gown down to hide the black on my nightgown beneath it.

"The machine belongs to a man named Joey Drew," he said.

"Joey Drew? Do you mean, like, Joey Drew Studios?" I asked, shocked.

"You've heard of him?"

"Of course! I watched the Bendy cartoons as a child at the cinema. You know, until this very moment I'd completely forgotten about that." Funny how certain childhood memories stay to haunt you forever and others just vanish as if that moment of your life had never happened in the first place.

"Well, it looks like Mr. Connor made the machine for Joey in New York but then brought it here to Atlantic City," said Bill.

"Why?"

"From what I understand they need to 'fix' the machine. It's broken. I actually helped Mr. Connor a few weeks ago on that. That's how I knew about the machine in the first place. I think they brought it here because the Gent company has unique facilities and connections in Atlantic City."

"Easier to bring a giant machine here than to send some Gent employees to New York?" I asked. That seemed very doubtful.

Bill shook his head. "I guess so."

"Or maybe . . . or maybe what happened to us wasn't weird. Maybe it had happened before."

"Maybe they had to get it out of New York, you mean," said Bill, following my train of thought.

"There was a monster trapped down there, Bill. It wasn't just living underground, it was purposefully trapped." I started to understand better what was going on. And it made me furious. "How dare they? How dare they bring a monster here, as if the people in Atlantic City don't matter like they do in New York? What is wrong with them?"

I sat hard on my bed, my brain swirling with rage. We all matter, and these men just thought they could bring something like this here and put all of us in danger.

"Well, they plan on taking it back to New York once it's fixed," said Bill, looking nervous now. Then again, lately he'd been looking quite nervous in general.

"And of course machines never break again. And does the

monster go with them?" I squeezed the edge of my comforter with my hands. I was boiling over but didn't have any outlet.

"What have you learned about the ink?"

That question helped focus my mind. I loosened my grip on the edge of my comforter. "I'm pretty sure I found a way to erase it, finally. I made a solution. It's in that vial there." I pointed at a stoppered test tube sitting in the little wooden stand that had come with the book. It was a dark crimson thanks in part to the iron oxide. The liquid was thick, similar in consistency to the black ink. In fact, with the texture and the color, it quite frankly looked a good deal like blood.

"You did?" He turned and looked at the vial. He seemed almost mesmerized by it.

"I also found out that the ink does something. It seems to enhance something deep inside whatever it makes contact with. For a little beetle trying to escape, it makes it manic and desperate." I watched as Bill gently picked up the vial. He looked at it closely. Examining it.

"I see," he said.

"I think it's had an effect on me, Bill," I confessed.

He didn't react. He didn't seem surprised. "Yes, that makes sense."

"It does?"

He turned and looked at me. "It's had an effect on me too."

Confessing to someone that

the deepest part of me was a coward had not been something I was planning on doing today. Or indeed ever in my life. But here I was, looking at Constance and knowing that the truth was not just necessary in this moment, it was vital.

"I'm scared all the time now," I said. "I think I've always been a little scared. Of what my future held, of being out of control, of the world. Never enough to feel it like when you read a scary book, but it was always there." Constance nodded. "Now I feel like running away all the time. I have run away. I ran away today out of the tunnel. I tried everything to make us run away from Brant . . ." I stopped. My throat closed suddenly. I felt like I was about to cry. I couldn't do that now; now was not the time. I focused my attention on the little vial filled with blood. No, it wasn't blood, I knew that, but it looked like it. It also scared me. I turned it around in my hand, watched the liquid run from top to bottom, from top to bottom, oozing as I flipped it slowly over and over again.

"I'm so angry," said Constance.

"I'm sorry," I replied, apologizing for my confession, for my bad behavior. I felt terrible. I was such a horrible person.

"No, I'm always angry," she said. "Like you. I think I've always had this need to be heard, to shout out, to feel understood. It's a lot."

I felt some small relief. She didn't judge me. She had her own concerns. Not everything was about me.

"So should we take this?" I asked, still staring at the vial. I didn't really want to. The red, the consistency, it all made me feel sick to my stomach. I looked up at her.

She shook her head. "I don't know. I don't know if it's safe. It cleaned my gloves, but can it undo these effects. Do we . . ." She paused. "Do we want to undo these effects?"

"Of course we do," I said. I couldn't live like this much longer. The battle not to flee every moment was getting harder and harder. "You must want to be yourself again."

Constance sat looking at her lap, her hands tightly grasping the cover of her bed. "I think this is more myself than I've ever been." She looked up at me. She looked scared. Almost petrified. She was shaking and I couldn't understand why.

"Isn't what we are experiencing just a magnified version of ourselves? You won't lose yourself entirely . . ."

"Bill, shut up," Constance said.

No one in my life except my father had ever said that to me. It made me freeze in place. Hurt but also frightened.

"Stay perfectly still," she said.

I realized then that she wasn't looking at me. She was looking just past me. Just over my head. Behind me.

I heard a dripping then. Like a leaking faucet. Drip. Drip. Drip. I heard it just by my ear. I felt nothing but pure terror. I couldn't feel my hands or my feet or my heartbeat. All I felt was a white-hot brightness inside me. A paralyzing, uncompromising level of fear that I had never felt in my life.

Constance rose very slowly, reaching out as she did, staring at whatever stood behind me. "It's okay," she said softly. But not to me. To it. I thought of the black ink under my chair in the corner of my room. The face outside the window. It was the monster. My mouth went dry.

"Bill, you need to stay still."

Well, that wasn't a hard instruction to follow.

"Hi," she said with a warm gentleness to the thing behind me. "We met last night, didn't we?"

The drip sound sloshed behind me now, like something was moving.

"Don't be frightened," she said. I wanted to laugh at that. Whatever was behind me was not the one that was frightened. "I'm Constance, this is Bill."

Whatever it was behind me made a strange soft moan sound.

"Are you hurting? Do you need help?" She started walking toward me, toward it. I held my breath, terrified that the sound would antagonize the monster.

The dripping behind me got quieter, as if it was backing away.

"You can stand now, Bill, but very slowly," she said, not making eye contact and continuing to move slowly toward us.

I wasn't sure I could, but I also knew I couldn't sit here with my back to a monster much longer. With all the will I could find, I forced the fear down, like swallowing burning bile in your throat. And I slowly stood, my legs shaking as I did. But I made it to standing and then I turned, keeping my head lowered. I didn't want to make eye contact with a beast.

Finally I raised my head slowly and saw for the first time a figure. Feet first, legs, then body, then head. It was a figure dripping in ink. As if an ink puddle had taken human form. It had no eyes, no nose, no mouth. The ink dripped off it continuously onto the floor and then was reabsorbed to do the journey all over again. It stood there, near the wall, near the shadows. It seemed to be staring at us.

The white-hot fear I felt dissipated slightly but now I could feel my heart thumping in my chest again, the panic rise, the desire to charge toward the door and run out of the apartment.

"What do you want from us?" I asked it. I wanted to sound calm like Constance, but my voice quavered.

It moaned again and then lifted up one of its inky arms. Raised it at us. A finger materialized from the ink. It pointed at me. Right at me.

"It's going to kill me," I said. I was light-headed; I didn't want to die.

"You want Bill?" asked Constance.

The figure almost seemed to shake its head. Slowly, it

moved side to side. And then the whole figure glided forward toward us. Toward me. It moved faster than I expected it would and then stopped, inches from my face. I could see the ink now, flowing in and out and around. I was mesmerized by it.

Suddenly the monster grabbed my wrist. I called out in pain. It held my wrist hard and raised my hand perpendicular to the floor. How could ink that had no substance still have substance to grab, to squeeze, to hurt?

"Oh my goodness, Bill. It wants the vial." Constance's eyes were wide with wonder. "Is that what you want? The solution?"

The monster turned its head to look at her, despite having no eyes.

"Give it to him, Bill."

It held my wrist fast. I couldn't open my hand. My fear was keeping my grasp tight around the glass. "I can't. I want to but . . ."

Constance was beside me then. In my ear a harsh whisper. "Do it."

"Don't be angry, I want to." I willed my hand to open. I couldn't.

"I'm sorry," she said, understanding then. Remembering my recent confession. "I'm sorry. You can do this. You are more than just your fear. Just like I'm more than my anger."

I closed my eyes but I could still see the monster in my mind. I opened them again and looked right at the creature. It didn't want to hurt me. It just wanted the vial. Just let go, just let go, just let go.

My hand opened suddenly and Constance gasped as the vial fell. The monster caught it—it moved so fast, so inhumanly. It turned away from us and I started to breathe again, light-headed from the air flowing through my body.

We watched as the monster stood there, its back to us. As it consumed the vial, glass and all where its mouth should have been.

"What happens now?" whispered Constance.

I shook my head. Words would not form.

The monster suddenly seized as if in great pain, bending over and against the wall. It fell to the ground and writhed onto its back, spasming and jerking around. I wondered if it was dying. I realized I wouldn't mind if it did. Just disappeared altogether, like a stain being erased.

There were a few more violent motions and then the creature curled up into the fetal position, lying on its side like a small child. I didn't care. I wasn't going to feel sorry for it.

Then it released a loud moan, a wail, a cry long and piercing, as if it was in great pain.

Then pop.

Just like that.

Just like Brant.

The creature exploded, ink flying everywhere. I turned to protect my face and held up my arms.

Then stillness.

"Oh my god," said Constance beside me.

"Is it gone?" I asked, not wanting to turn and look.

"No," she said. But she said it in a way that made me curious. Despite my horror, I turned to look.

On the ground lay a figure, a person. No ink creature. No monster. They moaned again slightly and rolled onto their back.

"Oh my god," said Constance again, this time bringing her hand to her mouth.

Knock knock.

Who's there?

Brant.

"Hi," I said.

They stared down at me with these looks on their faces. It made me laugh. Nope, still hurts. The one good thing about being an Ink Monster? No pain. Being a person again meant that the whole squeezed rib cage situation was back in full force. I took in a deep breath. Ow ow ow.

"Quick, help him onto the bed," said Constance.

Now I wasn't sure how they were going to accomplish that, so I shook my head and slowly started to push myself up. But instantly they grabbed me under my arms. I let them. Together we managed to lug this broken body to the bed and once again I was lying on my back.

"Your antidote works," said Bill as he sat next to me.

"It seems to do something alright," replied Constance, sitting to my right.

"Is there more?"

I saw Constance shake her head no. What were they

talking about? I had a flash of a memory then, of something red like blood, of reaching out for it, desperately needing it.

"I'll make more though," she said. Then they both seemed to notice my existence again. In unison they looked down at me. "Brant, how are you feeling?"

"Oh, swell, horse girl, swell." I closed my eyes and braced myself against the pain of speaking.

"This is impossible," said Bill from my left.

"Yeah, well, I'll be honest with you, Bill, old pal, it happened." I felt a rush of shame flow through me, which was good because it distracted from the searing pain. "Hey, gang, I just want to apologize."

"What on earth for?" asked Constance.

"Well, this whole situation we find ourselves in." I winced and grabbed at my side.

"Maybe you shouldn't talk anymore," she said, looking so wonderfully worried.

"Nah. Anyway, it's all my fault. I made us open that icebox. Followed you two where I wasn't invited. So I'm sorry." I was feeling a little light-headed now.

"Please don't," she said. "Let me get you some water." She vanished from view and I heard a door open and close.

I lay there with a thoughtful Bill staring somewhere in front of himself. The perfect view up his nose. Poor little rich kid. Finally he looked down at me again.

"What was it like?" he asked quietly, as if he didn't want anyone else to hear.

"Sorry, pal, what was what like?" I asked.

"When you were . . . that thing . . ." He was so pale, like a shadow of the fellow I'd known before everything had happened.

"It's hard to remember." I closed my eyes again, trying to look back. I saw only flickers, like still photographs in a book. Snapshots. There was a lot of darkness, but not like when the lights are turned out. It was a thick swirling blackness. Like being caught in a whirlpool in the depths of the ocean. Then there were moments of bright white light in the distance and moving toward it. Like how so many folks describe dying to be. But once I was at the light, I would suddenly be in a room. In a place I didn't recognize. I was aware then. I saw Constance. I saw Bill. I saw them and I knew inside that I was reaching out for them, trying to find them. Something inside me kept dragging me into that light. I don't know how I got to those places, I don't know where I went when I left. It was like a dream. Then tonight happened. It was too complicated for me to understand, and how to tell Bill about it? It seemed impossible. "I'm afraid I can't explain it."

Constance was back with the water. "Can you sit up, Brant?" she asked.

I nodded. "I can try." Once again they gently helped me and for the first time I felt a little more human. Feeling human was a really swell thing to feel.

Constance carefully handed me the glass of water and I took it. It felt so heavy to hold. There was so much substance to it. It was so . . . solid. It really existed in a really existing sort of way. I stared at it.

"Brant, are you okay?"

"Good question, horse girl." I took a sip of water. The cold ran down my throat. I felt it in my insides. It was fantastic. It tasted so good. Better than any soda or fancy drinks I'd ever had. I had the sudden absurd idea that I should bottle it and try to sell it. I was definitely still a little loopy.

"So," I said, holding the glass in both my hands, enjoying the cool feeling, "what's new?"

Constance smiled and Bill frowned and I felt like Dorothy in *The Wizard of Oz*, home at last.

"The machine belongs to Joey Drew," explained Constance.

"The animator, sure, that's interesting. Does that explain the ink?" I asked.

I noticed Constance glance at Bill and I turned to look at Bill's reaction.

"We hadn't thought of that kind of connection," said Bill.

"Okay," I said.

"They need to fix the machine and then bring it back to New York," Constance continued.

"And the monster?"

"*You're* not the monster," said Bill, more to himself than anything.

"I'm flattered you realize that," I said with a grin. The shame welled up again. I didn't know where this feeling of remorse was coming from. I never normally felt like this. I guess I always had some guilt, taking on a job that didn't make much money for my own ambition and not helping my family out more. Then of course there was what I was feeling right now, knowing I'd been lying to Bill all this time. But usually I could push those feelings down. "Say, Bill," I said. He looked at me. "I have something I need to confess. Feeling pretty ashamed of myself right now and I'm not usually one for humility." I laughed a little, trying to hide my discomfort. Then the sharp pain prodded my side helpfully.

"Well, that's no surprise," said Constance. "You see, that's the other thing we've discovered. The ink seems to have an effect on a person, seems to latch on to one's inner demons, as it were." She was looking so intensely at me. It was almost ridiculous. Then she said, "Unless that was a joke."

"It was and it wasn't," I replied.

"So evidently the ink makes me terrified and I'm going to just say this now to you two. We don't have time to catch up like this. We don't have time for any of this," said Bill, his voice actually shaking. It threw me. I felt really sorry for the guy.

"What do you mean?" asked Constance.

"What do I mean? These men are fixing the machine as we speak. I was with them. They want to move it soon. Joey said they want to move it tomorrow. I don't know if they're even still alive down there with that monster still roaming, but we have to stop them." Bill was almost panting now, speaking so rushed and out of breath.

"Well, that's what the authorities are for," replied Constance.

"Don't be absurd, Constance," said Bill. I felt a bit like I had an angel and a devil on my shoulders, debating each other for the moral high ground. It was kind of funny, but also exhausting to keep turning my head back and forth.

"Why? That's what the police are there for," said Constance.

"Well, maybe in other cities but here in Atlantic City they are his father's personal security system," I said, wanting a role in this performance.

Bill looked at me for a moment and then nodded. "Exactly. And it looks like my father and Joey are considering working together."

"Ah," I said. "The missing piece of the puzzle. Those men from New York—I thought they were the mob."

"I think they are also potential investors. I think Joey Drew Studios might be needing an influx of cash."

"The cartoons certainly are not as popular as they once were . . ." said Constance. She thought for a moment. "That machine, and all that ink. I wonder if it's a new way to make cartoons? Or maybe invent a whole new kind of a way of film-making we don't even know yet. It's definitely a new kind of ink."

"That's for sure," I said under my breath.

"So if we can't call the authorities, what do we do, Bill?" She sounded anxious herself, but also almost . . . annoyed.

"The machine needs to be destroyed."

There was complete silence then.

"Tonight," added Bill, in case we couldn't figure that part out.

"How do you propose we do that? We barely survived last time," said Constance, sounding even more frustrated.

"Fun story. I didn't," I added.

No one found that funny. Once again I felt ashamed. This ink was definitely doing a number on me alright.

"It's not 'we,' Constance. I have to do it. I'm the only one here who knows anything about machines, and it's my fault that the two of you were brought into any of this. And it's my father's fault that Joey has the money to make it work again. Besides," said Bill, "I fix things. It's what I do. I have to fix this."

"Oh, just stop it," said Constance. "I am tired of you boys thinking everything is about you. You might understand the machine but I understand the ink. So if this is the plan, I'm going to help you."

"It's dangerous," said Bill.

"I don't care. I want to do something that matters. Why won't anyone let me do something that matters?" She stood in a rush of anger.

"I'll tell you what," I added, "let me help. I bet I can walk. Probably." Another attempt to cut the tension with some humor, but again it failed. Tough crowd, as Bob Hope might say.

"Don't be foolish, Brant," said Constance dismissively.

"Hey, look, it'll make for a great story. Probably even above the fold," I said.

"What do you mean?" she asked.

"What?"

"What is 'above the fold'?"

I realized then what I had said. The shame flowed fast and furious. I was drowning again, but this time not in thick black ooze. I looked at Bill, who looked at me. The betrayal on his face was so easy to read, he might as well have written the word across his forehead.

"You're a reporter," he said in that question non-question way of his. "Of course you are. That's the only reason you wanted to be friends, isn't it? That's why you were there that night. You followed us. For a story."

"Look," I said, trying to prop myself up higher but slipping on the pillow, "yes, but I still think you're a swell guy, Bill. I think we are real friends even if the beginning was not . . . as real."

"I can't believe you. How could you do this to me?"

"Bill, when you think about it, it's not so bad. People meet in all kinds of circumstances. It's what happens after the fact . . ."

"You asked us to open that icebox. You did it for a story?"

"Well . . ."

"That's it!" Constance said, her voice loud and angry. "I will not listen to another moment of this. Are you both not aware that time is slipping away from us? Who cares if you're real friends or not? In what world does that matter when a monster is on the loose and a machine filled with ink that could destroy us all is being shipped to the largest city in America tomorrow?"

There was more silence, mine, at the least, filled with

mortification. And if what Bill had said was true about the ink's effects on him, I would not have been surprised at all if he wasn't completely terrified of Constance in this moment.

"You're right," he said.

I nodded in agreement.

"Good. So shall we go destroy the machine?"

"Yes," said Bill.

I nodded in agreement again.

"Good," said Constance. She took in a slow breath to calm herself and released it. "Now. Let me change out of my dressing gown."

CONSTANCE

You look just like Katharine Hepburn," said Bill as he held the taxi door open for me. He said it quietly, under his breath, like he was afraid he might be insulting me and also like he didn't want Brant to hear. I reminded myself everything he did or said would be tinged with fear.

"Thank you," I said. I didn't think I looked much like the famous actress, but I was wearing trousers and she was best known for her elegance wearing them. For my part, I just thought destroying dangerous machines would be less practical in a skirt. The aesthetics of the choice had not been on my mind.

"So this is where the world ends," said Brant, coming up beside us and staring with us at the dingy little bar.

"Hopefully not," I said. "Come on, lead the way, Bill. We don't have time to admire the scenery." Stay calm, I told myself, stay calm.

Bill nodded and led us inside and toward the back room. No one stopped us; there weren't that many people to do that anyway, but even the bartender didn't give us a second look. Did he know what lurked beneath him? Did he care?

We entered an empty back room and Bill put down his tool bag and carefully felt along the back wall. He stopped, smiled to himself, took in a deep breath, and pushed. The wood panel in his hands retreated an inch and then slid to the side.

"I hate secret entrances," I said, thinking about that evil metal door in the factory.

"I hate them more," replied Brant. We looked at each other and he gave me a wink. How he was standing upright in the first place impressed me, but that he was walking and joking was nothing short of miraculous.

"Let's go, let's go, let's go," ordered Bill frantically.

I flicked on my flashlight and walked through the hole in the wall. The floor sloped downward and I shone the light around the space in front. The tunnel in the distance was all darkness, but to the side there was a conveyor belt. Those bootleggers had thought of everything.

More light flooded the tunnel and I looked behind me to see Bill and Brant coming up beside me.

"Come on," said Bill, and he started walking down the tunnel. We followed, and I thought it was interesting how fear could also propel a person forward, not just hold them back. There was the fear of the thing. But there was also the fear of not doing the thing. In this case, I supposed, the fear of what would happen if we didn't break the machine. If it was taken back to New York.

We followed him down the tunnel, surrounded by the light of three flashlights. The darkness followed behind us and every once in a while I glanced back at the blackness, wondering if there was anything in the shadows. If the monster was stalking us and not the other way around.

I squeezed the fire poker I was carrying in my right hand hard, just to remind myself it was there. I wasn't entirely sure what I would do with it—I had never been taught how to fight. But I knew that the constant churning anger inside would tell me what to do.

The dark void in front of us turned suddenly brighter and brighter until we stopped in front of a wall. The tunnel forked now. We had a choice between left or right.

"Which way, Bill?" I asked, frustrated at his indecision. He was supposed to be our leader after all. He'd been here before.

"Left," he said, not sounding entirely certain. "Definitely left."

We followed him left, though as we turned I shone my flashlight right, just to see if there was any hint of a machine in that direction. All there was was more darkness.

We continued down the tunnel. Our flashlights highlighted sudden black voids in the wall, turnoffs down other tunnels. We kept going straight but I marveled at it all. At the size of this underground system. How had they built all this? Was it built to transport illegal alcohol, or had some of it existed before?

It didn't matter. None of my questions mattered.

All that mattered was the task before us. We had to do this. We just had to.

We reached another wall. Another fork in the road.

Bill stopped.

"Which way?" I asked again, feeling even more annoyed. This shouldn't be taking so long.

"I don't know," he replied.

"You don't know?" I asked. This was absurd!

"I didn't make it this far." He was quiet when he said it. Almost ashamed. He shone his light down one direction and then the other. "I . . . don't know." He did it again. "I don't know, I really don't know." The light started to shake, and I looked at his hand. His whole body was shaking. He was panicking. We didn't have time for this.

"Hey," said Brant, coming up beside him and putting a hand on his shoulder. "We follow the conveyor belt." He pointed with the light to the right and sure enough there was another conveyor belt along the far wall. Bill looked too. He nodded.

"Yes, that makes sense," he said.

"Lead the way," said Brant, giving him a friendly pat on the back.

Bill nodded and turned right. We followed him again. It

felt like we'd be following him forever. I couldn't take much more of this. My skin was itchy with frustration. I felt like a small child wanting to cry out, "Are we there yet?"

And then.

We were there.

Another wall, but not other tunnels. There was a door-shaped seam cut into it and a divot at hand level. Bill immediately figured out how to open it by sliding it to the left. So many sliding doors.

Then there it was. Right there. We were standing at the far end of the room, facing the far side of the machine.

Instantly my heart was in my throat as the memories came flooding back. I didn't want to think about any monsters lurking in the shadows so I quickly marched across the room and turned on the lights. They flickered to life and highlighted the familiar space. I looked around. I saw the icebox, the door still open. Well, they hadn't recaptured the beast, it seemed. Of course they hadn't. What incompetence.

"Well done, Bill," said Brant. Again Bill just nodded. "Why don't you sit down and rest for a moment."

"We don't have time for that," I said from across the room. How could anyone rest at a time like this?

"Yes, we do," replied Brant, giving me a meaningful look. Boys and their meaningful looks. Half the time they didn't even know what the meaning was, they just expected the rest of us to assume something profound.

"We really don't." I glanced at the open secret door.

There was nothing but blackness beyond it. No, not nothing. Somewhere out there lurked a monster that wanted to kill us all. If I hadn't been so scared of alerting the beast to our presence, I would have screamed in frustration.

Brant helped Bill to sitting, leaning him against the wall, then he walked over to me. I could see pain in every step he took.

"We can't let the ink win. Don't let your anger take over, doll."

"Don't call me doll," I said.

"I'm sorry, I won't again. Let him recover. He can't do the work properly. It'll take less time this way. You know that's true."

I understood what he meant, but it felt impossible to just sit and wait for Bill to get over the fear that he could never get over. Just like I would never get over this rage. When we finished all this, I'd make another vial of the solution. I'd fix us. I could fix things too.

I walked over to the machine, to what I had decided was its front with the giant open pipe like a gaping maw. I stared at the black ink coating the inside, up into the darkness and shadow.

"Don't touch it!" called out Bill from his spot on the ground.

"I'm not going to," I said as calmly as I could. I had no intention of touching the machine. I remembered that night clearly. I remembered Brant reaching up inside and then the sound of the monster. A monster that must still be on the loose somewhere.

"What do we do, Bill?" I asked.

Bill was just sitting there like a lump, looking at the ground. He took in a breath and let it out, and did it again. He was wasting time; he was being indulgent. He was being a rich kid who had never had actual real-world troubles fall onto his shoulders until now. And now that it was happening, he couldn't face them. Ink or no ink, this was who he was. I couldn't stand it. I wouldn't stand for it. Why was I sitting here waiting for him to make all the decisions? I had a brain too. I knew what needed to be done. We needed to destroy the machine. It was as simple as that; we probably didn't even need Bill in the first place to do it. Breaking things is so much easier than fixing them, after all. I marched to the other side of the machine where the long pipe curled. I raised my poker, and with a loud guttural cry from somewhere deep within me, I stabbed into the side of the machine.

"No, Constance, no!" called Brant.

The spear pierced the metal. I was shocked when it plunged deep into the machine. I hadn't really anticipated my plan would work. I thought I wouldn't be strong enough, or the metal of the machine would be impossible to penetrate. Black ink gushed out and rained down on me. I pulled hard on the poker and dislodged it, falling backward onto the ground. I watched as the ink with its strange fingers groped its way along the floor toward me. I scrambled away from it, staring stunned at the mess I'd made.

"Constance, are you alright?" asked Brant, limping over and bending down at my side.

"I'm fine, I . . . didn't think that this would happen. I was just . . . angry." I was shaking now. My turn, I supposed. What had I done?

What had I done?

All of it was my fault. This wasn't some deep inner demon lying to me, trying to keep me here paralyzed, unable to move, to breathe. This was the complete truth. If I hadn't offered to work for Gent, if I hadn't brought Constance down here, if Brant hadn't seen us and followed, none of this would have happened. The monster would have stayed locked up. Mr. Connor and Joey Drew and whoever else worked for them would have fixed the machine and taken it away. It would have been like it had never existed. All of us could have continued our lives and been quite happy.

As the ink sprayed out of the machine and started to pool around us, I wondered if I should just drown. If it would be best if I allowed the ink to take over my body and to explode like Brant had.

"I'm sorry, Bill; if I can't control it, why should I expect you to?" Constance's mournful apology echoed around me, like she wasn't really there, like a spirit talking to me. "Please, Bill, you need to help us."

264

What help could I be? I fix things. What a joke. I destroy things, just like my father. I pretend to be something grander than I am.

"Bill, come on, buck up!" It was Brant now, echoing in my ear. They were here. They were right next to me, but they felt so far away.

"I can't. It's a lie. I can't fix anything. I destroy everything."

I could feel Constance right near me but I couldn't look up at her. I just stared at the ink pooling, reaching out, searching for us.

"But that's the good news," said Constance. "We need you to destroy the machine."

I sat with that information. I realized it was the truth. I finally looked up. Constance was covered in black specks of ink, Brant was holding his side, it was time to do this. I slowly stood up. I could feel my whole body go numb. I couldn't tell if it was supporting my own weight or not. But I was upright.

"Your tools, sir," said Brant with a fancy accent, like he was my butler. I wanted to explain that that's not how butlers sounded but that was not the point. He was trying to make me laugh.

I made my way over to the other side of the machine, carefully trying to avoid stepping in the puddle of ink that reached out to me as I passed. I made it to the side panel I'd helped Mr. Connor with, sat down, and wrenched it off. It was a nice feeling not having to worry about being delicate and careful. Destroying things took a lot less effort than fixing them.

"Can we do anything?" asked Constance, crouching next to me.

"Keep a lookout," I replied. "For Mr. Connor and Joey."

"And the monster," added Brant.

I hadn't wanted to say that part out loud.

I was left alone then; the world was only this small square foot in front of me. I took my wrench and looked around inside for any bolts I could undo, or even just loosen. It was dark inside the machine, harder to see than last time, so I turned on my flashlight.

"Bill, you have to hurry," said Constance, standing by the secret entrance.

"I know," I said.

"No, it's not like that. The shadows, they're back."

I looked up. The room was getting darker. The fear rose up to my fingertips, my hands were shaking again. Droplets of sweat appeared on my brow. Focus, Bill, focus. If I just undid all the work inside, if I could remove that lever . . . I worked as fast as I could, but even with my bright flashlight, I could feel the shadows creeping in.

Suddenly, the lever was loose in my hand. I pulled it from the machine and placed it next to me. Next I grabbed the gears behind it. Soon enough, I had a small pile of machine guts on the floor beside me. I grabbed them and shoved them into my tool kit, then I stared into the bowels of the beast. Was that good enough? It didn't feel good enough. It definitely wasn't good enough. I felt this surging fear, this need to eviscerate the whole machine, to turn it inside out.

My flashlight glinted on something then. I looked close,

almost stuck my head inside the machine. A shining chrome tube heading up into the bowels of the beast. It was small but significant. Made of a different metal than the rest of the machine, it had to be important. I picked up my wrench and started at the fitting where it began to bend upward.

There was a sudden roar that nearly stopped my heart. It was nothing like a lion or a bear; it was almost more like a scream, a high-pitched scream with a low rumble under it. It chilled you to the bone. I looked up. The room was pitch-black. I couldn't see Constance or Brant, just the beams from their flashlights.

"Where is it?" I asked, my body paralyzed once again. I didn't have the strength to fight the terror inside me anymore.

The beams from the flashlights raced across the room, searching.

"Find it!" I ordered. I returned to the pipe. My hands were shaking so much, I couldn't hold the wrench in just one. I dropped my flashlight—what was the point anyway?—and with my two hands twisted down hard.

There was another loud roar, this time just above me. I looked up again and grabbed for my flashlight, swinging it away from the machine and upward. I screamed.

My beam landed on a wide toothy grin. Sharp teeth loomed above me. Like the Cheshire cat's smile, just floating there. But I knew there was a body too, I knew the monster had claws. It looked at me, or at least seemed to. I was paralyzed. I couldn't run. I couldn't turn off the flashlight.

"Bill, get out of there!" I heard Brant call out.

Yes, yes, get out of there. Get out of there, Bill.

What about the pipe? My right hand still held the wrench tight inside the machine, but I couldn't look away.

The mouth seemed to grow wider and it opened, revealing the sharpness of its teeth.

Then something very strange happened. All the fear, everything, it was gone. I felt this lightness, this feeling of acceptance. I looked down and saw the ink pooling around me. I saw it climb up over my legs, pull itself up onto me. I suddenly understood the phrase "foregone conclusion." I turned to the machine, my hand steady as a rock. I pulled hard at the wrench, at the pipe fitting. I felt an explosion of ink cover my hand as the chrome pipe fell and I caught it deftly. I tossed it out of the machine with its other guts. I looked up at the monster once more.

I win.

"Bill!" called out Constance.

And then Brant: "Constance, no!"

Constance, it's okay. It's really okay. I stared at the beast's wide-open mouth. The light glinted off the monster's glistening ink body. Thin, just a shadow. All my life I'd been afraid of what my future might be. But here it was, staring me in the face. As the ink rose up my torso, I felt warm, I felt at ease.

I looked up at the creature.

And for the first time in a very long time, I smiled.

41: BRANT

I held Constance, flailing in my arms. I could barely hold her back, she was strong and determined. She had rage on her side, and her anger at me for preventing her from helping poor Bill. But I had my shame, my inky shame, and it made me hold her tight. Because if we couldn't save Bill, then at the least I was going to save us.

He was just sitting there. He could have run. He could have fought back. But he just sat there. We watched as the ink grew up his body. Up his neck. He sat there, smiling like a darn fool. Just smiling. The beast smiling back at him.

And then the beast's mouth opened wide, so wide, dislodging its jaw, teeth glinting in the light.

Constance stopped struggling in my arms. We both just stared.

And watched.

As Bill smiled, the ink crawled up and over his head just as the beast lunged down at him.

"No!" cried out Constance, but I was speechless. For once. I had nothing to say. How was this happening?

The inky figure exploded as the beast enveloped him.

"You monster!" screamed Constance, and she turned to me. "Let me go now, Brant." It was an order but I couldn't do it. I didn't know what she was going to do when free anyway.

"He's not dead," I reminded her. I recalled my own experience, the swirling and the bright lights. He would be searching for us, for help. If he didn't give in to the pull of the blackness. It was a powerful pull. But maybe he could resist. "I know what it's like. And you can bring him back, just like you did for me!"

That seemed to calm her down.

"I can make some more of the antidote," she said, piecing together what I'd said in her own mind.

"Exactly."

The monster roared suddenly and we turned back. I held Constance tight, not really to protect her, but just out of a primal personal fear. We watched, frozen, as it seemed to notice the open door to the tunnels. It slowly stalked its way toward it, stared for a moment, and then disappeared through it.

"Oh no," said Constance. "No! We have to stop it!"

I let her go and said, "Yes. *I* do."

She looked at me in complete disbelief. "Don't be a hero. I can help."

"Of course you can, but you need to escape, you need to make the antidote. So let me show this knucklehead who's boss," I said with a smile. I wasn't feeling nearly as confident as I was pretending to be. I had no idea how to fight a monster, but I felt I understood it better than she ever could. I knew at least what it was like to be a dripping inhuman creature.

I walked slowly toward the pool of ink where Bill had been. The light in the room was coming back now that the monster had gone. I stood over his toolbox and saw the pipe wrench lying there. I picked it up. The ink climbed over my fingers.

Constance came up to my side.

"I'll take his bag. Let's put the pieces of the machine inside. I'll get rid of them," she said. We bent over and together put everything back in the bag. Something sharp pricked my finger.

"Ow," I said.

"Are you okay?" asked Constance.

"I'm okay." Once again I felt deep embarrassment. It was just a cut. I wasn't being eaten alive, say. "So we have a plan," I said as we stood up and Constance held the bag close to her body.

Constance nodded.

"No matter what happens, you have to keep going, you hear me?" I asked. I had to get through to the reasonable part of her, past her ink-fueled rage.

"I hear you."

We walked slowly to the tunnel, her holding the bag with her fire poker all in one hand, me with my pipe wrench. We shone our flashlights down the tunnel; they glowed bright and we knew that meant the monster was far ahead of us, somewhere.

We didn't say anything to each other—our plan was simple and stupid. I glanced down at the pipe wrench in my hand. Would this thing be enough against an Ink Monster? Probably not. I laughed to myself. It was all so absurd. I noticed something then. I held up my hand so I could see it better, pretending I was examining the wrench even closer.

I laughed again. Of course. Of course.

Constance looked at me. "What?" she asked.

"This whole thing is pretty funny when you think about it," I replied. I couldn't tell her the truth. My little cut was bleeding. Which wasn't really a big deal. Except the blood was black and I had a pretty good feeling it wasn't blood at all.

"No, it's not," she replied.

"Let's go," I said, lowering the wrench, and we walked slowly into the dark tunnel.

We stepped back into the darkness. We were hunters tracking a beast. Never would I have imagined that I'd end up here. After all of this. A pretty swell story. Not that I'd ever get the chance to write it.

We were so quiet, both of us. We were listening and looking. The darkness was empty in front of us . . . for now.

"If anything happens, you have to run. You can't fight, got it?" I whispered, reminding her. I knew that her anger wanted to definitely do the opposite, but she couldn't.

"I know," she said. She sounded obviously annoyed with me and instantly I wanted to apologize. But this wasn't the time or the place.

"You run without me. I need to get it back into the room and trap it in there if I can't, you know . . ." I stopped. The idea kind of scared me.

"Kill it," she said, finishing the sentence. I guess the idea didn't scare her as much. She had moxie, this dame, that's for sure. Maybe she should have been the one to take on the beast. I didn't know how much time I had left.

I could feel it inside me. I could feel the ink in my veins. Should I tell her the truth? That the antidote was only a short-term solution?

"The light's getting dim," whispered Constance.

I hadn't noticed, but I saw it now. Our flashlights didn't seem to fill the tunnel with quite as much light. I sucked in my breath slowly,

"Are you ready?" I asked. The light dimmed further. "There's a branch in the tunnel right there, you see it?" There was a dark hole in the wall; it was her best possible escape. These tunnels all had to lead somewhere.

"I see it."

"Good."

The light dimmed again.

Here we go. This was madness. But weren't we all mad here?

"If anything happens," I said.

"No more apologies," she replied in that curt way of hers.

"Well, just wanted to say it was gosh darn swell getting to know you."

There was a pause and then she said, "You too."

She didn't know how I was feeling. She thought we'd make it. That we'd both make it. She didn't know that this was it. That this was good-bye. Forever. That was for the best. I didn't like good-byes much personally. They never felt satisfying. They never quite did the job.

The light went out.

"It's here."

There was a sudden roar and the monster was on my back, pushing me onto the ground, I could feel its strange wet skin, its claws ripping at my shirt. The ink in my veins seemed to pulse and rush through my body faster. I gasped as I landed hard. But I was able to cry out into the darkness: "Constance, run!"

I struggled on the ground and finally was able to twist my body and swing the pipe wrench and hit the monster right in its face. It howled and stared at me, barely even flinching, and pulled back almost in confusion, giving me a moment to spring upright, blocking the tunnel's exit. I swung at it again, and it staggered backward, tilted its head slightly at me almost like it was surprised. This was good. This was very good.

I glanced around. Constance was nowhere to be seen; that was good too. She was off. She was safe. Someone had to make it out of here, and she was a pretty swell someone. I was struck across the face and flew up against the wall of the tunnel. I noticed in that small moment that one of the creature's hands was smaller than the other. Interesting. I pushed myself off the wall and came at the monster swinging.

"Come on, you!" I shouted, flailing wildly. Every inch of my body screamed out in pain, not just my ribs, but my insides, they just wanted to burst through my body, burst out like a bubble. I felt like I was holding on to my skin like a hat that wanted to blow away in a storm. But I couldn't give in.

The monster seemed to know something was going on inside me. It lunged and it fought back, but it didn't bite, and it didn't claw, and I fell again onto the cold stone ground. It stood above me and roared so loud I thought my eardrums would burst. There was no way I could defeat this beast in a fight. But there was one thing I could do.

I swung upward with all my strength. The pipe wrench hit its mark a few times, causing the creature to howl and slink backward and stop again for a moment and stand upright staring down at me. Once again it seemed confused, wondering why would I tap it gently with this small metal thing. But it was enough of a pause for me to pull myself up and make my way through the beast's legs and start running. Come on, follow me, you inky devil. I heard it behind me, coming for me. Good. I just had to get it back to the machine room. I just had to get it there. Then I could let go, I could just let go.

I ran. I ran fueled by rage and

fear. No, I told myself, not fear. Nerves. Like Lily called them. Make it a positive. I turned down the tunnel. I had no idea where it led to, all I knew was it led away from the monster. But it also led away from Brant. This was so unfair. He was in danger again. He was putting his life on the line again, so soon after I had brought him back. I was the one fueled the most by this situation. I was the one who ought to be fighting the beast. My stomach lurched, as if it was trying to pull me back toward him. Before it was too late. Before I lost him. Again.

No. I shook my head to get rid of those thoughts. Even if the worst happened, I could save him. I had the antidote. I'd save Bill, I'd save everyone.

It was incredibly difficult to run with any speed, holding this bag full of tools and bits of machine, as well as the poker and the flashlight. I hobbled along feeling ridiculous and annoyed that I couldn't just sprint. But what could I get rid of? Certainly not the flashlight, nor the poker. And the whole point was for me to dispose of the bag. I couldn't just leave it in a tunnel for any of the Gent people or this Joey Drew fellow.

Joey Drew cartoons.

That's what this was like. I was running in a cartoon, the walls of the tunnel passing me by, all the same, never ending, carrying an absurd number of props with me. How was this real life?

I skidded to a sudden stop at a fork. There was no conveyor belt to tell me which way to go. I looked left, then right. Then just stared straight ahead. No, I wouldn't be intimidated by this choice. I would use logic to get there. I took a step to my right. There was nothing to see but more tunnel. I could feel a knot form in my stomach. So I closed my eyes and listened. I strained to hear something, I didn't even know what, but maybe there was something. I smelled too, though all I could smell was that strange tangy ink. I could feel the drops moving across my skin, trying to find some way to take me over, but I wouldn't let them.

Then I opened my eyes and stepped to the left. I strained again to hear something, anything.

Waves. Did I hear water lapping? Did I smell salt in the air?

I wasn't some hound dog, I couldn't tell these things for sure, and my mind was desperate, so maybe it was all just in my head. But it was enough for me to choose the left side.

I started running again. I didn't feel tired, even though my muscles ached. I felt grateful for my rage. It spurred me on. It made me want to get out of here, and most importantly it made me confident that I was right in all my decisions. I knew this was probably problematic in the real world, but in this strange underground world, I was like Alice from the book. This wasn't reality.

It was Wonderland. I was falling down a hole except I was running along it and the hole was sideways.

We're all mad here.

I heard waves now. I heard them properly, not just maybe. I picked up speed, holding the bag tightly to my chest. I ran toward the sound, and then the smell, the smell of air and salt and the outside world.

"I'm coming!" I called out as I raced forward.

I was almost there, I could feel it. I could feel it against my face, my skin. I was almost there.

Something yanked me hard from behind. My head snapped in a whiplash and I fell hard onto my back, dropping everything in my hands. My flashlight rolled, shining now from behind me. I sat for a moment in a pure shock that quickly turned into rage. I reached for the poker that was just too far away for me to grab. I saw a shadow along the wall, a creature. The monster? No. It seemed to have two long ears. Like a rabbit, or possibly some kind of dog. But it was tall and human sized. And fleeting.

The shadow vanished down the hall. It left me. It had attacked me and then left me. I didn't understand.

I turned to look at the mess around me. I watched as the poker rolled away from me a few inches and then suddenly vanished.

I heard the waves louder now. Quickly I reached for my flashlight and shone it ahead of me. I stayed on the ground, crawling slowly forward. The sound of waves came rushing back and I was very aware of my surroundings suddenly. I wasn't in a dream, I was in a tunnel built by bootleggers in the 1920s. It was all very real.

I crawled forward and then saw the edge. The ground just ended, stopped without any warning. Impossible to see in the dark. I lay on my stomach now and snaked forward, the rough ground scratching through my shirt to my skin. I reached out and curled my fingers over the side with my right hand and pulled myself. Slowly but surely I came to the edge and looked over.

There was water down below, rushing and crashing into a cavern. It was maybe thirty feet down, with rocks protruding. I scanned my flashlight over it all and wondered why this place existed. What purpose could it possibly serve? Then it occurred to me. High tide. I shone my light into the dark void to my left. That wasn't more cavern, that was the sea. That was the outside world. They could ship out the whiskey from here, load the boats up. I wondered if that's how they got the machine here in the first place.

Was this the way out? Did I simply wait? I had always had patience in the past; my whole life I had had to wait for things. I had had to wait on people, wait for quiet moments to finally be with my own thoughts. But now I thought I had run out of it. How on earth was I meant to harness a power that I resented so thoroughly now? I itched at the thought.

I looked over my shoulder into the darkness. That long-eared thing had saved me from going over the edge. It hadn't attacked me. It had wanted to help me. What other creatures were in the darkness? Were they all somehow attached to the machine, drawn to it like a magnet, or did they live inside it only to be released when we opened the icebox? Or when I pierced the pipe? Or at some other point we hadn't connected yet to everything? Was there a science that could explain it all?

No. There wasn't. And who cared? This was dangerous and careless. This again was a certain group of people making decisions with no care for the rest of us. I picked up the tool bag and stood slowly. I felt a renewed confidence and stood on the edge, my toes just over the water far below. I held the bag in my arms and then I took in a deep breath, I harnessed all the rage I had inside me and I flung it into the churning water beneath me. I watched it fall into the waves and disappear instantly.

I felt a weight lifted. That, at least, had been done. Now I had to do the other thing. And that was to escape.

"Help me!" A voice shouted in my ear. I was once again grabbed from behind and this time yanked around to find myself face-to-face with a man with crazed eyes. He was soaked in ink, but I could still see he was in coveralls with the word "Gent" sewn onto it. The name Scott was there too, underneath, inky marks partially obscuring it. He wasn't an ink creature, he was human. But he seemed more animal than anything.

"Help me! It's after me, you have to help me!" He stared at

me with wild eyes and then looked over his shoulder and back again. My scientist brain took over and managed to keep me calm, even holding my anger at bay despite my desire to fling his hands off me. I told myself his behavior was likely the ink's effect on him, targeted his paranoia.

"I'll try. Do you know the way out?" I asked, trying to control my temper. How could I possibly help him when I couldn't help myself?

"There's no way out," he replied, shaking his head. He repeated it again and again.

"There is though. There's the way through the bar. There are other tunnels," I said, trying to prick a memory of his. He had clearly lost his mind being lost down here with the monster for who knows how long.

He kept shaking his head. "No, no, no. You can't help. No one can help. It'll kill us all." He sank to the ground. He reminded me now of Bill. Sitting there. Just staring at the beast. Not fighting back. It made me so angry.

I turned to the water. I walked to the edge once more and looked down with my flashlight. The rocks were jagged but there was some empty space. Right below. A small pool's worth. Like a small pool to dive into on a horse. It's easier to dive into the water without a horse, I told myself. Much easier.

I turned back to Scott. "We should dive," I said. "I think we can make it."

He sat at the edge of the light. He shook his head. "No, no, no."

"Come with me," I said. I'd wanted to sound kind and soft, but it came out as a gruff order.

He slowly crawled away from my outstretched hand. Shaking his head. Shaking his head. Shaking his head.

Until the dark enveloped him.

I stared into the darkness, listening to the sound of an echoey "no no no" as he retreated back down the tunnel. Until it was gone. All I heard were the waves crashing below.

Suddenly a giant screaming roar of agony rumbled through the tunnel, vibrating my very bones. The monster. Had Brant killed it? Was that the sound I'd heard?

I remembered my task. Part one was done, I'd gotten rid of the machine parts. Part two, get home to make the antidote.

Time to get the job done.

I turned and faced the churning water below. I shone the flashlight down and examined the small area that seemed safe. Straight down. That's all. It wasn't far.

The water churned. I stared down at it.

I closed my eyes.

Keep your head down, Constance. Do the job.

Get it done.

BRANT

I had managed to get it to stalk me to the entrance, and I was exhausted at our cat-and-mouse game. Any adrenaline that had been pumping through me, hiding any pain I was feeling, had now decided to unveil it like a special surprise dessert at a fancy restaurant, "Ta-da!" And it was unbearable.

I swung at the monster and it grabbed the pipe wrench with its hand. It was fed up with my little toy, I could tell. I didn't have the strength to yank it out and instead it flew up out of my hand, hitting me under my chin, knocking my teeth together hard. I fell backward, onto my back, hitting my head with a dull thud. I lay there, trying to catch my breath, and reached up to my mouth. I could taste blood. But it wasn't salty. It was different. It was familiar. I withdrew my hand and looked at it, sure enough black ink. I was oozing from the inside out. My ears buzzed.

I was so close and yet so far away. I felt entirely ashamed. I had one thing to do, just one. I was brought back for one night to do it. One night only. I laughed. I was feeling that strange drunk feeling again, light-headed and silly. "For one night only, Brant Morris versus the Monster of Ink, tonight at the Top Hat Nightclub," I said out loud. I laughed some more.

Then I closed my eyes, I felt that pull, I could see the swirling blackness, I wanted to give in and melt away. I wanted to seep into the cracks of myself. The feelings were so familiar now. I'd been through this once before. No. No, not yet. I had to get up. I had to just finish this. I opened my eyes again.

Looming over me was the monster. It was so close to me that I could feel its stinking breath on my face. I could see right into its mouth, past its sharp scissors like teeth and into the blackness. I didn't know what it was doing but I stayed completely still. I didn't want to move an inch.

Slowly it pulled away from me, standing at its full height. My fingers carefully felt around the ground for the wrench. I touched something metal. It was a little too far for me to grasp. The monster opened its mouth wide, its jaw distended, teeth sharp. He let out a piercing roar, the sound made your blood run cold.

I kept trying to grab at edges of the wrench. I glanced over at it and with all the will left in my body I lunged for it, just as the beast lunged down at me.

And a dark figure lunged at it.

Flying over me like Superman was a figure from nowhere. It tackled the monster by its legs and the monster teetered, slightly unsteady. The figure rolled out of sight and the monster turned, engaging with it. It let out a massive roar. I then watched the figure rise and race into the machine room, the monster hot on its tail. I sprang to my feet, adrenaline coursing through my body for one last hurrah.

I stood and grabbed at the door, ready to slam it shut on the monster when I saw the figure. Inky black, dripping, like a form of a person but with no features. It stood and turned to me for a moment. I swear it was looking at me. Then I thought. Was that me, was that what I was, what I was to be again? It was like looking into a mirror and a time machine all at once. I didn't want to close the door anymore. I wanted to help it. Fight the monster alongside it.

Then it gave me a nod. A nod. It was so human. It was like it knew me. Recognized me.

"Bill?" I asked.

The figure turned back to the monster and lunged at it again. It was futile. The monster was huge, but it was enough of a distraction that I managed to slam the door shut and lock it, heart thudding in my chest. I stood in the dark tunnel. I felt completely spent. Over. Done.

I turned my back to the door and slid down it. There. I'd done it. No, *we'd* done it. Thank you, Bill. I wondered if when I returned to that inky form, if I'd be able to communicate with him again.

Were there others? Were there folks in New York who had come to a similar fate? We had done our best to prevent it happening again. But had it already happened? Was it too late?

If there were others, I thought as I closed my eyes, at least we wouldn't be alone. We could be lost in the wilderness together.

Constance, I hope you made it.

It was time. My body knew it; my mind knew it; my heart knew it.

Time to be invisible.

Time to let go.

CONSTANCE

I took a moment to just lie there.

To look up at the stars and shiver in the cold. To breathe. Then I sat bolt upright. I stared at the ocean, dark and foreboding. I didn't have the time to gather my thoughts. I had to get back to my apartment, to my home. I had to make the antidote. I had to save everyone.

I stared along the thin strip of beach I had landed on. I couldn't quite say I swam here. The current had taken me. The waves had pulled me back. I had fought my way out of the cavern and into the wide, never-ending ocean. And I had eventually wound up here. On a shallow rocky beach that sat next to the highway just up the brown grassy hill. No cars had come by. I was so very alone.

I stood up, shivering. I didn't know if it was the cold or the shock or the fear. It was probably all of it. I burrowed deep within myself and found my rage waiting patiently for me. I released it into the wild and I screamed. I screamed so loudly that I thought my voice would carry over the waves forever.

Then I stopped and bent over, hands on thighs, panting. Enough.

It was time to go.

I marched up the hill and started my long walk along the road. I hoped for a vehicle to come by. I hoped for some kind of help.

I walked and walked. No lights, no houses. Just a girl alone in the dark. Walking. Her wet trousers and shirt frozen in the cold air. Her hair just long icicles.

Just get home. No matter how long it takes. Even if you freeze to death. But hopefully before that happens.

The night was so long and so dark. The sun would never rise again. All was cold and endless. I was despairing, I was angry at the world for everything. For the machine, for the ink. For all of it. At least we stopped it. At least we fought back.

Bill.

Brant. Was Brant alive anymore? Had he been consumed? I feared the latter. How could it not be?

Even if I could make the antidote, how would I ever find them again? Would they still be trapped below that ground or would they find me? Like how Brant did before? Yes, I would wait for them, I would wait for them to find me and when they did I would be ready. I would devote the rest of my life if I had to, to bring them back.

There was a light. A brightness behind me. It lit up the dark road in front of me. I turned, and all I saw was brightness. I shielded my eyes.

A car.

It slowed.

I took a step to the side, wary. I had hitchhiked before, but it was always a bit of a risk. You never knew.

The car seemed fancy and the passenger-side window rolled down. A pleasant enough–looking man stared at me for a moment.

"Are you alright?" he asked, looking concerned.

"Just cold."

"Well, do you want a ride?" he asked.

"I'm going to Atlantic City," I said.

"So are we. Hop on in!"

I was so cold, and so tired. I laughed then to myself. I thought of the danger I had just been in, the life or death of it all. If I could face that, I could face anything.

I opened the door and slipped inside, closing the door behind me. It was warm.

I also wasn't alone.

"There's no escape," said Scott from Gent, staring at me wild-eyed. "You can never escape."

I stared at him.

"Oh, don't mind him. He's harmless," said the man in the passenger seat. He turned around to look at me. He extended a hand back toward me. "I'm Joey," he said.

I stared.

"No escape," said Scott. "No no no no no . . ."

The car sped off.

THE MACHINE

Swirling blackness wrapped so tightly, at first like a hug and then it squeezes, it crushes, it smothers. It feels like fire but it's also cold. It burns. Cold can burn. A quiet buzz, then louder, like a thousand voices talking at once. Screaming at once. Outside and inside. Our thoughts are not our own thoughts. Whose thoughts are these? How many of us are there? How many more will join us?

We are all screaming. We are all waiting. We are all . . . lost.

The light appears in sudden bursts. Too bright, it pierces at you, tears you apart even as you reach out for it.

What is there to reach for? Why hurt yourself? Just sink back. Sink back in with your friends.

Fear. Bill.

Shame. Brant.

Anger. Constance.

We sink back and back and back. We understand now. We see how all this time we were wrong. We understand the joke now.

Knock knock.

Who's there?

We can't fix the machine. We never could.

Knock knock.

Who's there? Who is there? Out there? Out here?

We're all here.

We understand now.

It's the punch line to the joke:

You can't fix what's not broken.

ACKNOWLEDGMENTS

I want to thank my agent, Jess Regel, and my editor, Lori Wieczorek, along with everyone else at AFK Scholastic, for all the amazing help and support with this book. I also have to thank my parents who are always there for me (go Team Kress), my guys, my husband, Scott, and my cat, Atticus, for being awesome. And of course the Meatly and Bookpast for allowing me to play in their world in the first place. I will always be so grateful for the opportunities you have given me!

Lastly, but certainly not least-ly, to all the Bendy fans who have been utterly amazing. I absolutely could not do this without you!

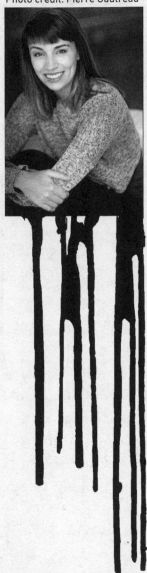

ADRiENNE KRESS is a Toronto-born actor and writer. Her books include the award-winning and internationally published novels *Alex and the Ironic Gentleman, Timothy and the Dragon's Gate,* and *Hatter Madigan: Ghost in the H.A.T.B.O.X.* (with bestselling author Frank Beddor), as well as Steampunk novel *The Friday Society* and the gothic *Outcast.* She is also the author of the quirky three-book series The Explorers.

Bendy and the Ink Machine: Dreams Come to Life was Adrienne's first foray into writing horror, but as an actor she has had the pleasure of being creepy in such horror films as *Devil's Mile* and *Wolves.* And she took great pleasure in getting to haunt teenagers in SyFy's *Neverknock.*

Find her at AdrienneKress.com.

Twitter/Instagram: @AdrienneKress